KV-638-975

JR RETURN

MONTANA HIT

Unknown to each other, two hard-cases were heading for the isolated settlement of Judgement Creek, one of them on the run, and the other on the prod for vengeance. Their trails cross in a twisting drama of love, hate, double-crossing, cowardice and murder, played out against the wilderness of nineteenth-century Montana territory. At the centre of it is the long-standing, respected sheriff — a lawman who is, as yet, untested.

CHARLES LANGLEY HAYES

MONTANA HIT

Complete and Unabridged

LINFORD
Leicester

First published in Great Britain in 1993 by
Robert Hale Limited
London

First Linford Edition
published 1996
by arrangement with
Robert Hale Limited
London

British Library CIP Data

Hayes, Charles Langley
  Montana hit.—Large print ed.—
  Linford western library
  1. English fiction—20th century
  I. Title
  823.9'14 [F]

  ISBN 0–7089–7826–6

uLu 16·9-99

Published by
F. A. Thorpe (Publishing) Ltd.
Anstey, Leicestershire

Set by Words & Graphics Ltd.
Anstey, Leicestershire
Printed and bound in Great Britain by
T. J. Press (Padstow) Ltd., Padstow, Cornwall

This book is printed on acid-free paper

SL 28\10\99

For
Dave Whitehead and Ben Bridges,
and memories of Frontier City

Prologue

I REMEMBER the chinook of that spring for two reasons. It had been a bad winter that year, the worst they said in living memory. Then the chinook had come, the warm wind from the north, heralding the spring, melting the Montana snows. How a wind coming down from the ice-clad Canadian Rockies can bring warmth was beyond the understanding of a nine-year-old. In fact, a lifetime later I still don't understand. But, ain't no gainsaying, it does. And with the chinook comes the warmth, the sun, the green shoots, the blossoms. And all the promise of a new season.

But that year the chinook brought something else too. It brought a man called Heller to town. I'll never forget him either. I ought to have known at the time, with a name like that. Heller,

the man from hell. *A hell of a name.
And he was to have one hell of an
effect on my life. Of course, I didn't
know that then. That was to come. All
I knew, he was dirty and mean looking.
Even a kid like me could see he spelled
trouble . . .*

1

AS he came out of the pass with the mountains cutting a jagged line against the evening sky behind him, he reined in and absorbed the view. A rutted wagon road descended five hundred feet to a nest of shacks, smoke spiralling from cranky stovepipes. He turned and looked at the roughly carved sign beside the trail. JUDGEMENT GULCH. The name seemed to mean something to him because he nodded before nudging his blanket-covered gelding down the grade.

Although the snow piles along the trail were thinning, marking the end of the winter, it was clear the man had seen cold times up in the mountains. He wore a muskrat cap with the flaps still tied tight under his unshaven jaw and the collar of his sheepskin coat was high round his neck. He made the descent one-handedly, his right arm hanging slack by his side.

Reaching town he slowly rode the length of main street until he saw a two-storey frame house labelled HOTEL. As he dismounted a ragged-furred dog came hesitantly from the boardwalk. It made to sniff at the newcomer's heels in curiosity but its investigations were terminated when the man grunted and lashed out with a mud-spattered boot.

The stranger looped the reins over the hitching-rail and entered the building. The grubbiness of the sparsely furnished lobby was compensated by a glowing stove.

His heavy feet on the roughly planked floor brought the proprietor from the back. Around the same age as his visitor, he was gangly-tall, feet spread out at angles, and had a long horse face with lips that, also like his visitor, had never been taught to smile.

He looked the traveller over, noted

the twisted right hand. "You travelled far, mister?" he grunted by way of greeting.

The stranger used his teeth to pick the mitten off his good hand. "Far enough," he said, warming both the good hand and the crook one by the stove. "You got a room, a meal and a place for muh hoss?"

The other went behind the desk. "Surely have. Five dollars a day. Payment in advance."

"Five dollars?"

"The only hotel in town. Includes horse feed and a hearty meal for your goodself."

The visitor undid the fastenings of the hat under his chin and put out his good hand. "Gimme the key and tell me the room."

The horse-faced man hesitated. "Rule of the house. Payment in advance."

The traveller moved from the stove. "I don't do business that way. I pay when I'm satisfied. Now do you give me a key or do I have to come round there and take one?"

The proprietor breathed deep and took a key from the board behind him. "Room number one," he said weakly. "Can't miss it. First at the top of the stairs."

The visitor took the key and began to mount the stairs, paused after a couple of steps and turned. "What's the name of the sheriff here?"

"Adams, sir. Sheriff Adams."

The man rubbed his stubbled chin. "I thought it was Bolan," he said gruffly.

"No, sir." The proprietor looked askance for a second, then realization crossed his face. "Oh, Bolan's the sheriff down at Judgement Creek."

"What's the name of this place?"

"Judgement Gulch."

The visitor emitted an expletive.

"Common mistake," the hotel man observed. "We often get the mail mixed up. Ever since I lived here there's been talk of changing one of the names but the town councils can't agree which is gonna do the changing. You know, local pride."

He laughed weakly but the other was more interested in local geography than local history. "Where the hell's Judgement Creek?"

"About twenty miles along the rimrock."

Voicing another expletive the visitor turned and continued up the stairs.

★ ★ ★

Heller slung the soogans to one side and rolled out of bed. In his longjohns he crossed to the window hugging himself with his good arm in an attempt to retain some of the warmth. He cleared a peep-hole through the frosted pane and looked out. Still dark in the valley but morning sunlight was just beginning to shaft through the peaks. He kicked into his pants, punched his good arm through a shirt sleeve, then manoeuvered his dead right into the garment. He completed his dressing

7

with his boots and outer clothing. He put on his muskrat hat. He could move the injured right arm and use the crook fingers of the claw hand enough to tie down the flaps. He'd had enough experience in making the most use of what he had remaining on the end of his right arm. Pulling the black leather glove on to the claw hand he made for the door.

After going out to the lean-to out back and fixing up his horse with a bagful of oats he returned some ten minutes later to the main building. The bleary-eyed proprietor was dropping eggs into a sizzling skillet. "Morning, mister."

Heller threw away a meaningless grunt as he passed through. He went upstairs and came down with his gear.

"You're litting out then?" the other said, seeing his guest's burden.

"You're mighty clever," Heller said, dropping on to a chair by the table to face the platter of eggs and bacon. "You been to college or something?"

After that, his meal was finished in silence. He wiped his mouth, rose and made to pick up his warbag.

"That'll be five dollars," the proprietor said. "Like we said."

Heller halted in his movement and gave him a look that had trouble printed on it. "Like *you* said." He put his good hand into a pocket and pulled out some coins, dropping them on the table.

"That ain't fair, mister," the hotel man said, looking at the dollar and few nickels and dimes.

Heller picked up his warbag. "It ain't a fair world."

"You're some dollars short there," the proprietor persisted, not knowing from whence he summoned the courage.

"All I got," Heller said, moving to the door. He grinned. It was the first time the other had seen him offer anything resembling a smile. But there was nothing pleasant about it. Despite his disability and already encumbered by his warbag he adroitly opened the door. "Tell yuh what, pissant. If I knock off a stagecoach or bank and I come back this way, I'll throw you a few dollars as I ride through." And he was gone.

Minutes later he was riding out of Judgement Gulch, heading along the rimrock. It was still cold. During the night the vestigial fingers of winter had groped their way down the mountain and still held their grip, reluctant to recede in the morning air. As he cleared the town he noticed a telegraph pole and it suddenly occurred to him that, in his tiredness, he'd said too much to the bozo of a hotel keeper. He reined in, pulled out his six-shooter and shot away the porcelain holder. The wire fell, cutting a groove in the snow.

2

"**I** ASK you to raise your glasses and toast the happy couple," the mayor of Judgement Creek said loudly, hoisting his own glass high at the end of his speech. John Adrian Newcomb, timber merchant and mayor, was a big man, expensively dressed with a colourful vest encompassing the beer-big roundness of his belly. Taking their cue from him the rest of the gathering rose, glasses aloft. On the top table alongside the mayor, Laurie Bolan looked somewhat embarrassed while his wife Jessica averted her eyes altogether, choosing to look at the tablecloth.

"To the happy couple," the dignitary went on, a sentiment that was vocally echoed around the room. In unison the assemblage sipped ceremoniously from their glasses then, in more staggered fashion, they lowered themselves to their seats. The Stockman's and Cattleman's Market Saloon, known to locals simply as 'The Market', had been closed to regular trade for the evening, cleaned up and decked out with tablecloths.

The room was full, indicating the popularity of Sheriff Bolan and his wife, now being helped to celebrate their tenth wedding anniversary. It had been eleven years since Laurie Bolan had ridden into Judgement Creek and taken over the town's drapery store.

Then in his early thirties, he had thrown himself into the business. He had made no bones of the fact it was new to him but he had worked hard and learned the trade. The townsfolk were warmed by his genuinely happy surprise at his success and his discovery of latent skills. It was no secret that in his early life the young Texan had tried his hand at a variety of jobs without finding his niche. In frustration he'd headed out to Virginia City attracted by the silver boom. Then, on the point of giving up after years of prospecting, he'd hit a vein. Rather than remain after the vein was exhausted, frittering his money away while he searched for another lode, as is the way with panhandlers, he'd had the horse sense to ride out with full pockets. He'd grasped his opportunity and travelled north-west to start a new life with his grubstake in Montana Territory.

For him, opening the drapery store in Judgement Creek had been an experiment, a complete change of trail for him, but it was clear he'd finally found his forte. The shop had done well. He had then used his continuing prosperity to expand and now his business interests included hardware and dry goods stores. Within a few years he had risen from a trail-dusty stranger riding in, to become one of the town's prominent figures.

He was a good-looker with clean-cut features and a pleasant, easy-going nature that meant he became liked by everyone.

And particularly liked by the young

lady he employed as manageress of the drapery store. Jessica was the daughter of Phil Perry, Welsh Phil they called him, one of the town's early settlers. The two young people began walking out together, and Welsh Phil was more than happy to give his consent when Laurie asked for his daughter's hand in marriage. Following their wedding, a big affair with all the townsfolk attending, Jessica took over responsibility for the running of the drapery store, eventually becoming more involved with all the stores. Although a simple girl with no more education than was prevalent at the time in the wilderness of Montana, her understanding of business grew in concert with the expansion of the settlement. Although her main interest was the drapery store, in time she had become conversant with the operation of the whole of the small but thriving Bolan empire.

Her weighing heavy with child within a year might have complicated the arrangements. However, the whole town was involved in their relationship, so when it came time for her confinement there was no shortage of local ladies willing to help with the store.

The result, little Johnny Bolan now nine, was at this moment sitting with his parents enjoying the festivities at their tenth wedding-anniversary party in the Market Saloon.

But Laurie Bolan, the mild-mannered man behind a counter, had clearly got something in his constitution belied by his appearance. The lawless days of Judgement Creek might have long gone but, half a dozen years back, passing rowdies had gotten into a fracas in the saloon and one of them had put slugs into the incumbent sheriff when he'd been called to the scene by an irate saloonkeeper. It had happened that Bolan had been taking a quiet drink at the time. And, of all the saloon's patrons, it had been he who had faced up to the rowdies. At that time, although there was an element of civilization in the settlement, Montana Territory itself was still a wilderness where it was wise for even a storekeeper to carry a gun. And thus it was, Laurie pulled the unused Colt from the holster under his frock coat. The threatening maw of a gun coming from such an unexpected quarter enabled Laurie to get the drop on them, allowing the townsfolk to herd the miscreants into jail.

However, the sheriff died overnight from his wounds and when news got out, a crowd of angry townsfolk started to congregate outside the jail. At the centre of it was Barney O'Hagan, one of the old-timers who still believed the townsfolk should dole out their own justice. By morning the gathering had become a lynch mob out for vengeance and, with no effective control, they broke into the place and dragged out the gun-happy stranger.

Before long the erstwhile gunman was hanging from the cottonwood at the end of Main Street. Of course, when the dust had settled and folk had calmed down, there was lots of guilt about. But then a more practical matter came to the fore when they realized the town was without a law officer. At an emergency meeting of the town council it was mooted that the job be offered to Bolan. When it was put to him he had demurred at first. He was a fancy-dressed businessman. He'd learned a few things in his life; what he didn't know about material and cloth was nobody's business. But a lawman?

Why not? they had argued, putting it to him that his action in the saloon had been a clear demonstration of the fact he had the qualities for the job. His businesses were established and could be run largely by delegation.

Judgement Creek was still a relatively small settlement, the councillors maintained, and, with the exception of the previous night's shooting, generally law-abiding, so the job of law officer would not be all that demanding.

Indeed, for most of the time it would be no more than a part-time responsibility.

Laurie talked it over with Jessica. She was apprehensive and he was surprised when, after some consideration, she recommended he take the post. She had grown up in the town, seen it quieten down, and seen how peacekeeping had become a mere daily round. She also knew her man. Now his businesses had become routine she had noticed he was becoming fiddle-footed, on the look-out for something new. A few years as law officer would give him a new interest, a new challenge, and could well be the stepping stone for other things. It would get him on to the town council for a start, and then maybe the mayoralty. And so it was, he had accepted the job.

Tonight in the Market Saloon he felt good. "You know, Jessy," he said, pouring some wine into his wife's glass, "I'm sure a lucky man. What with you, Johnny. A comfortable living. And the friendship of all these people."

"They've taken you to their hearts, Laurie," she said, laying her hand on the back of his. "And I'm lucky too," she went on, "to have such a man as a husband. Kind, considerate. And the most handsome man in town!"

Raising his arm and dropping it around the back of her seat, he allowed his hand to flop affectionately on her shoulder, as he looked around the room at the familiar smiling faces. There was Red, with his ginger hair, long down his back like a woman's; but a real man underneath. A stockman, he owned a spread the south of town. Although like Laurie always finely dressed these days, there wasn't anything his punchers could do that he couldn't. Next to him, Pete, owner of Judgement Creek's only bank.

Both Pete and Red were self-made men with businesses they'd worked up over the years so that they virtually ran themselves, allowing the men now to spend time in town in each other's company. And there was nothing better that they enjoyed than a game of cards along with Ade Newcomb, the mayor.

Pete caught Laurie's looking his way and raised his glass in salute. As Laurie smiled and raised his own glass in acknowledgement, another man rose at the far end of the room. He crossed the open space, carrying a large bunch of flowers. There was a roll to his walk as though the floor was moving, a habit he'd acquired during his days at sea.

"For you, ma'am," he said, presenting the bouquet to Jessica.

"Why, thank you, Roy," she said, accepting them and looking them over with evident pleasure. "Where did you get such a variety at this time of year?"

He winked a roguish eye. Roy the Boy as he was known, had ways of organizing anything he put his mind to. A former ship's cook, he now ran the local eats-house and had organized the food and cooking for tonight's spread. "From me and the lads," he said in his clipped English voice, pointing back at the far table.

A group of young men waved noisily and raised their glasses. Deaney, Miff, Spud and others. Most of them family men now in their thirties, they had once been the rowdy youngsters of the town and hadn't broken the habit of regular drinks together.

As Roy returned to his seat, Mayor Newcomb leant over and exchanged some words with Laurie. The lawman nodded and the mayor got to his feet, banging the table with a spoon. "Your attention once again, ladies and gentlemen, if you please."

It took a while for the chattering to subside, then he continued. "As you all know, I'm thinking of retiring soon. Time to hand over the reins to a younger man. I know many folks think elections are a helluva bore, so I'll make it easy for you and this is an opportune time to share my thoughts with you. I can't think of a better candidate than Laurie, so

I'm recommending him to you, good people. That'll save you all having to think about the choice. I've had a word with him and he tells me he'll be happy to run for the office when the time comes."

A bout of clapping broke out.

"I'm sure it'll be a runaway win for him," the mayor went on, when the applause had died down. "The guy don't have an enemy that I know of."

Jessica looked at her husband, his clear blue eyes, neat black hair. "He's talking about you," she whispered, smiling and clasping his hand.

"Naw, he's gotta be talking about some other bozo," Laurie whispered back.

As the mayor continued with his eulogy Barney O'Hagan rose from his seat and made for the lavatory. When he had emptied his bladder he went outside, stood on the boardwalk and took out matches and cigar. Do's like this had been rare in Judgement Creek, but folks were getting more of them now the place was civilizing up. He enjoyed the booze and the food but he didn't cotton to the mayor speechifying. That he could do without.

There was a chill in the air but he could suffer it for a few minutes. Anything but listen to Adey Newcomb rambling on. That he should be standing outside at such a time was not accidental. He was an insider and an outsider at the same time. The cosiness of the town's inner circle irritated him. Occasionally when he got likkered up he would assert himself and take matters into his own hands. As he had done that night when he had led the mob in breaking down the door of the law office. It had been he who had fixed the rope around the man's neck and strung him up to the cottonwood at the end of Main Street. Jehosophat, had that been a hanging.

He lit the cigar and contemplated the taste. With his buck teeth and his turned up nose exposing his nostrils, he looked like one of the rats that crept in and stole the feed from his grain store.

Stretched out before him in the clear moonlight, the town was quiet. He had come to Judgement Creek in the early days. It had started life as a huddle of trappers' shacks when a person could stand in one place and see deer, elk and buffalo, all at the same time. For a while it had been a man's town with nothing but a saloon and brothel. That's when he had arrived, starting a business to supply grain for trappers' horses and pack animals. Then the first settlers made it up the mountain trails in their prairie schooners and the first thing they did after building their own shacks was put up a church. Then came the traders with their stores. Last year they'd got around to building a school. That had came last because there wasn't any profit in it.

He stepped back and listened at the door but the mayor was still droning on.

3

INSIDE the Market Saloon, the mayor took a drink to lubricate his throat before continuing with his praise of the sheriff "No, siree. There ain't many folks you can say that about. A man going through life just making friends. Especially somebody wearing a badge. We all seem to cross somebody some time or other. Even an easy-going, virtuous man like myself!"

Laughter and friendly jeers rippled round the room.

"He's a man experienced in business and peacekeeping," the mayor continued, "and he knows the workings of the town. After the long term of service he's put in at the law office, good service you'll all agree, I know he'll welcome the chance to exchange his badge for the seat at the head of the town council's table. You all know the murmurings coming from territorial capital, about Montana's application for Statehood. One of these days it's gonna come about and we need good strong leadership here, to see that we get a good deal out of it. I'm sure that when the time comes our Laurie will do us proud."

As the mayor returned to his seat to the accompaniment of clapping and voicings of approval, the bartender shouted, "Coming, Manny!" and resumed his task of weaving in between the diners with his drinks tray. The man looked out of place amongst the finery, with a round woollen hat clamped tightly on his head. A Jew known to everyone as Manny, he had lost the skull-cap required by his religion and, such an item of headwear being difficult to obtain this side of New York, he had to make do with the woollen cap, which was permanently in place. Folk had thought he was called Manny because his name was Emanuel, that is until someone found his given name to be Isaac. The truth was he was called Manny because that was the name he used to address everybody else, irrespective. Some kind of Yiddish humour, some claimed. Others guessed it was more simply because he just couldn't remember folks' names. But he was the ideal man to have behind a bar, with a benevolent face and a smile or a wink for anyone.

Swirling adroitly between the chairs he paused to let a man pass who had risen from a seat at the far end of the room. A tall fellow with round pixie-like cheekbones, he walked ungainly with drink until he got to the top table, where he leant forward to breathe beer fumes over the mayor.

"What can I do for you, Deaney?" the mayor asked.

"I don't know if you remember, Ade," the young man said slowly with jocular affront, "but you asked me and Moe to give you a few tunes here. You know, you being the mean bastard you are, to save you having to fetch a full orchestra all the way from Miles City."

"Yes, yes, of course."

"So, Adey, ready when you are."

The young man returned to his place and groped under the table for a fiddle case. Then he beckoned to a friend and the two of them went to the end of the hall to join a third positioning himself at an old upright piano.

A few minutes later the mayor rose again. "Ladies and gentlemen, your attention please for the last time. It is now time for some dancing. So, after the happy couple have taken a spin you may all take the floor with your own partners."

He gestured grandly to the musicians who struck up something that eventually took the semblance of a waltz.

The mayor sat down and raised his eyes in invitation to the honoured couple. After some persuasion Laurie managed to coax Jessica on to the floor and they danced around the room to applause, her embarrassment only declining when other couples ventured forth.

After a set of waltzes the fiddlers played a reel during which Laurie and Jessica partnered his deputy, Norman, and his girlfriend. Norman was not the best of men for the law business, without the forcefulness of character needed to stamp his authority on situations which was what peacekeeping was all about. But Laurie suffered him. Like his girlfriend was suffering the young man's clumsy feet during the reels.

A few energetic dances later Laurie and his wife returned to their places. Jessica dropped in happy exhaustion into her seat and looked at Johnny. Her young son was fighting a rearguard action to keep his eyes open. She put a gentle hand on his shoulder. "I think it is time you were in bed, young man."

"Oh, Ma," he whined. "I'm not tired. Really."

"You've said it, Mother," Laurie

said, winking at his wife. "He is a young man now. He's had a glass of champagne. He's stayed up late. Later than the kids in town. He is a young man. And that means he's big enough to put himself to bed if he wants."

The boy perked up, excited at the prospect of putting himself to bed like an adult, something he'd never done before. Now alert, he nodded by way of endorsing everything his father had said. "If I'm grown up, can I curse too?"

"No," Laurie grinned. "Any ill-mannered bozo with half a brain can do that. That's not a sign of growing up. That's something else you learn as you grow up. Well, Son, you gonna go home and bunk up by yourself or are you gonna wait until you've fallen asleep and your Pa has to carry you home?"

"Naw, that's for kids," the boy said, summoning up last reserves of wakefulness. "I think I'll hit the sack."

Laurie grinned at the attempt at manfulness in the voice.

"Very well," his mother said. "Give me a kiss then."

After the boy had done so and been sent to say his goodbyes to the rest of the company, which he did adroitly shaking hands with each, Laurie took him to the door of the hotel and helped him on with his coat. "See you in the morning, Son."

As he watched the boy set off along the boardwalk he really didn't know when he'd been happier.

Back inside, there was an interval in the music playing and Laurie took the opportunity to talk with the leading fiddle player. During the day Deaney ran the livery stable.

"You sure you're gonna be OK for getting the horses ready at the crack of dawn, Deaney?" Laurie asked, noting the bleary-eyed look in the man's eyes.

"Don't you worry, Mr Bolan. What I say, I does. Don't matter if I'm likkered up tonight. Tomorrow is another day."

Laurie shrugged philosophically and returned to his wife.

A couple of hours later the festivities were over and only Deaney and his die-hard pals remained, trying to empty a remaining beer barrel. Laurie and Jessica stepped down from the porch of the now darkly lit Market Saloon. With the husband's arm pulling his wife close, they strolled dreamily along the trail, the short distance out of town. The air was crisp, the stars pinpoints in the clear night sky.

They reached their home and walked up the path. Even in the moonlight, it could be seen to be a house of substance, large, two-storeyed with dormer windows.

She stopped on the porch. "Kiss me."

For a while they embraced silently.

"Quiet," he said, as he opened the door a little later. "We don't want to wake up the young man."

"It's been a wonderful evening," she

murmured. He closed the door and they walked across the thick, patterned carpet he'd had shipped over from England. He dropped into one of the deep leather chairs while she went upstairs to check the sleeping boy.

She returned and sat on the chair arm beside him. "You were right, what you said earlier," she murmured, leaning her head on his. "Our son is growing up fast before our eyes."

"Yes," Laurie said. "And big enough to do without us for a few days."

She pulled away from him. "What do you mean?"

"I'm taking you to Miles City tomorrow. It's all fixed up. Norman's looking after the law office. Your folks are having Johnny."

"What for?"

"A second honeymoon. And you can spend all our money in the fancy stores they have there."

Her eyes sparkling with genuine surprise, she hugged him. "When did you arrange all this?"

"Couple of days ago.

"I didn't know."

"'Course you didn't. Told everybody to keep quiet about it because I wanted to surprise you."

"Laurie, you're an angel."

4

WHEN Jessica awoke, Laurie was already loading the buggy. She heard voices and looked out of the window. Light was only just breaking and Deaney had already brought two horses over from the livery. He'd fixed one in harness and was roping the other at the rear as relief. She shook her head as she turned away to begin her own preparations. How the ostler could be up so early after the drink she'd seen him put away she didn't know. By the time she was washed, dressed and downstairs, Laurie was returning from having checked his deputy was OK in the law office. After she and her husband had taken Johnny to her parents' house, the couple installed themselves on the drive seat.

All set, Laurie gigged the horse and Jessica nuzzled against her husband in the heady, crisply-cold air as they settled to a steady gait out of town. Clear of Judgement Creek they followed the meandering trail that ducked and twisted through small ravines, past streams burgeoning with melted snow-water while, in the distance, regal mountains brooded.

★ ★ ★

It was mid-morning in the Market Saloon when Ade Newcombe entered. The place had that morning-after feel. "Howdy, Manny," he said to the barman.

As permanent as the woollen cap on his head Manny always had a smile breaking out from the full black beard that decorated his face. The permanent smile broadened. "Hi there, Manny. Usual?"

"Yeah. I trust Laurie and Jessica got away OK this morning?"

"Yes, sir." It was Deaney the ostler, leaning on the far end of the bar. "Saw

36

'em off personal at sun-up."

"That's good," Ade said, taking his drink over to a table where he sat down and lit up a cigar to wait for his card-playing pals.

A few regulars drifted in, parked themselves. It was quiet for a spell, like the place itself had a hangover, and it stayed that way until the door opened to reveal a bear-sized man with an eye-patch who entered and stamped the coldness out of his feet on the boards. He had big features matching his physique, thick lips, a splodge of a nose. His one intense, serviceable eye, stared out from under an overhanging forehead.

He raised his hands as he approached the bar. "Drinks all round, Manny," he bellowed in a thick accent. "Max is back, *mein herren.*

The occupants welcomed him in varied ways, nodding, raising a hand. Max was a big man of German stock, who spent most of his life as a trapper alone in the northern wilderness. He took off his beaver-tailed hat and shook a head of long, shaggy hair.

"Good hunting?" Manny asked, pouring from a bottle of schnapps kept especially for the trapper.

"*Ja*. And got a good price for stuff too." He would disappear for a month or two, then return to town with his merchandise. He could see more out of his one eye than most men could out of two and always returned from his hunting trips with a train of pack-horses overladen with best quality furs. Until he ran out of money he would focus his mind on drinking and other important things such as reading, smoking, philosophizing, and watching the grass grow outside his little shack on the edge of town. A man dependable and as solid as the mountains over which he'd spent a lifetime roaming.

He threw back his drink and waited for Manny to top up the proffered glasses along the bar. "You missed a good party last night, Max," the bartender went on, replenishing the trapper's glass. "The sheriff and his wife, celebrating their wedding anniversary. Real good night."

"Ach," the trapper retorted. "Would like to have been there. Laurie, he's one good fellow. Get him a drink on me when he comes in."

"It'll be a spell, Manny," said the bartender. "He's taken his missus to Miles City for a second honeymoon."

The trapper made a ribald gesture with his arm. "And all I got for company is wolves and bears."

★ ★ ★

Laurie and his wife hit the Yellowstone late afternoon, and followed it downstream into Miles City. Swollen by a myriad of feeder streams by the time it had reached the town, the river had become a thing of majesty, sweeping like molten glass past the settlement on its way to the distant Missouri. Birds, for whom the water was a hunting ground, skimmed the surface. As the couple's buggy rolled past a jetty a man in a roll-necked riverman's jersey waved a greeting.

Well back from the bank could be seen a line of false-fronts, stores servicing the river and its traffic: fishing trackle, boating gear. Trading centres for furs. Stores selling hunting gear. Others specializing in provisions for the steady flow of pioneers aiming further west.

Along the main drag Laurie made enquiries about a good hotel; they found a suitable place, the Crown Hotel, and registered.

They began the next day with a good breakfast, then set out to explore the town. It wasn't long before they came upon a gentlemen's outfitters. Jessica looked over the merchandise in the window and, despite her husband's protestations that he wanted to buy garments for her, insisted they begin their purchases with clothing for him. She selected material and he was measured for a suit. Then he stood to one side while she stacked up items on the counter: shirts, socks, neckties and shoes. He felt warm knowing she was enjoying herself picking out things for him. Back home, he already had a packed clothes closet but, what the hell, it was only money. Eventually she looked at the pile and nodded, satisfied.

★ ★ ★

His arm around a stanchion, Johnny Bolan sat on a rail, his legs swinging rhythmically over the edge of the boardwalk. It was like an adventure, living at his grandparents' house while his folks were away. His grandma had given him some money for the candy store and he sucked on a stick as he watched the traffic drifting up and down the main street of Judgement Creek.

His lips puckered reflectively around the candy as he studied a rider just coming in. What had caught his interest was the man's right hand, hanging loose at his side, covered in a black leather glove, its fingers held in a permanent grasp on nothing. He was fascinated to see the man dismount and one-handedly tie his mount's reins to the hitchrail. He watched the newcomer step up on to the boardwalk and ask some question of a lady passer-by. Then the young boy remembered he had been told not to be too long and, with no other thoughts of the stranger, dropped off the rail and skipped back in the direction of his grandparents' house.

"Obliged, ma'am," Heller said, touching his muskrat cap to the lady who had given him directions to Laurie Bolan's house. Five minutes later he was standing at the gate surveying the imposing structure, spacious, gable-roofed, solid. He nodded at some thought, then opened the gate and headed up the path. It took several raps on the door before it was opened by an old lady. She wore an apron and had a feather duster in her hand.

"Morning, ma'am," he said. "I'd like to see Sheriff Bolan. I'm told this is his place."

"That's right, mister, this is where he lives," the lady said, looking the visitor up and down, "but I'm afraid he's away. I'm just the cleaner. Can I take a message?"

He ignored her question. "Away? What d'you mean?"

She didn't like the look of the man or his attitude. "He's gone away with his wife."

He looked puzzled. "What's that all about?"

"Don't see as it'll do any harm telling you. It's common knowledge. They're having a holiday to celebrate their wedding anniversary."

The man grunted as he took in the news. Then, "When's he due back?"

"They didn't say. Could be a few days, could be a week. It's a carefree thing. Kinda second honeymoon. No

43

precise plans for time of return. Look, mister, I'm busy. Like I said, can I take a message?"

He shook his head and forced a smile. "No, ma'am. Thank you kindly. It's personal. Him and me, old friends, you know. I was just passing through and had a mind to look him up. Where've the happy couple gone?"

The woman still didn't like the man, but maybe appearances were deceptive and if he and the sheriff were friends there was no harm in telling him. "Miles City."

"Obliged, ma'am." He touched his hat and turned. She watched him walk down the path, then returned to her chores with no further thought of him.

★ ★ ★

Ade Newcomb entered the telegraph office and took a letter from his pocket. "Steve, I want you to send a wire to Miles City for me."

Yes, sir," the agent said, turning a

leaf of his pad and licking the end of his stubby pencil.

"I got some business correspondence here and I need to query it with the customer." The mayor ran a lumber business up the valley and was preparing a consignment for a customer in Miles City.

The clerk wrote down the message and took his pad over to the transmitter. He pressed the button but there was no sound. "Hell," he said. "Line must be down."

"You sure?"

"Yes, sir," the clerk confirmed, vainly tapping the device again. "See for yourself."

"OK, let me know as soon as it's operating," the mayor said and opened the door.

He wasn't to know that someone had a habit of using telegraph fixings for target practice.

★ ★ ★

Heller had been riding for the remainder of the day when he caught sight of a river in the distance. That would be the Yellowstone and meant he must be close to Miles. Exhaustion tugged at his brain as he paused by a rill of clear, snow water. Seems like he'd spent a lifetime traipsing this darn country. Now it was getting dark, cold, and he needed a place to hole up. He could probably make the city but in such a place lodgings would be expensive and he was almost out of jack.

Hell, nothing for it but to press on. He gigged his gelding and had gone no more than another half-mile when he saw a lone rider ahead. He pulled in again. The other hadn't seen him yet. He tugged the rein and manoeuvred his mount behind a stand of fir just up from the trail. Through the whitened foliage he watched the rider advance.

He could have blasted the critter clean out of the saddle but as he neared he could see he was nothing but an old-timer, stiff in the saddle,

46

squinting at the world through a pair of square-cut glasses. Harmless.

When the man was almost level Heller pulled out his six-shooter and nudged his horse to descend. "Hold it there, mister!" he shouted.

The man pulled in as Heller drew up before him. "Hands in the air," Heller went on.

The man nodded dumbly and raised his hands.

"You got a wallet or a purse?" his accoster asked. Heller wasn't bothered about weapons. If the man had a side-pistol it would be under his thick overcoat, impossible to get at and be any use in the circumstances. The oldster didn't seem to be too competent in the eye department anyway.

"Yes, sir."

"How much?"

"Mebbe forty dollars."

"Show me, but no tricks. I could have dropped you way back, still can if you give me cause."

The old man fumbled at the front of

his great-coat and pulled out a leather wallet. He opened it and exposed some bills.

"That'll do," Heller said. "Toss it on the ground."

He watched the man drop the thing on to the hard earth of the trail. "What's your name, old-timer?"

"Ben Whitehead."

"Well, Mr Whitehead, I figure we got some understanding here. Now, get the hell outa here before I change my mind about turning you into a carcass for the grizzlies hereabouts to chew on."

A look of relief showed on the aged features as the road agent sheathed his gun and nudged his own horse to one side to allow the man wider clearance with his. Heller watched him disappear along the trail before picking up and counting his loot. Almost fifty dollars. That would grubstake him for a fair spell.

5

JESSICA came out of the small changing-room and shyly paraded for her husband.

"A mite short, ain't it?" Laurie said. The emerald skirt was almost shockingly narrow round the hips and legs, and finished a foot from the floor revealing ankles, a flash of calf and a touch of petticoat frill.

"All the fashion out east," the proprietor said proudly.

Laurie nodded non-committally, taking the word of the expert.

"You think it's too daring?" Jessica asked, looking down as she spun for her husband's appraisal.

"It'll sure-fire open a few eyes back in Judgement Creek," he chuckled. "But," he went on, "if that's the coming thing and it takes your fancy, it's yours, Jessy."

"But what do you think, really think?"

He clicked his tongue and winked. A beaming smile replaced the apprehension in his face, and she walked over to him and clenched his hand.

"Now what about coats and hats and things?" he went on.

"Oh, yes," the proprietor said, turning to open another cabinet. "We have a wide choice available to complete the ensemble."

Fifteen minutes later there was a stack of ribboned cardboard boxes on the counter. Laurie returned a much depleted wallet to his pocket. "OK. You can deliver those to the Crown Hotel?"

"Certainly, Mr Bolan. No charge. I'll get a boy on it right away. And a very good day to you, madam, sir."

Jessica hugged her husband's arm as they walked through the store doorway.

"Now to find something for little Johnny," he said when they were on the boardwalk.

"I saw a store down the block with toys in the window," she said. "They ought to have something he'd like. This way."

From a distance Heller had watched the couple go into the fashion emporium, and then he had taken up a waiting position, leaning against a stanchion. He was glad to see, on their exit, they walked towards him. He watched them advancing and when they were ten feet away he stepped in their path. "Sheriff Bolan, I believe."

"Yes?" Laurie said in surprise, focusing his eyes ahead.

"I've come a long way, Sheriff."

There was a pause before Laurie spoke. "Heller."

"That's right, pal. And it's taken a lotta searching."

Laurie's face changed. Silently he took Jessica's arm from his and, without taking his eyes off the man, he nodded at the store doorway to their side, as an indication for her to move out of the way.

"Laurie, what is it?" she asked, doing as she was told, her face ashen.

He ignored her, keeping his gaze on the man before him. "You done a lotta searching," he said by way of challenge to their accoster. "So what?"

"It's cards-on-the-table time, Sheriff," Heller went on. Every time he said the word 'sheriff' it was with a disdained emphasis. "Like I says, I've waited a long time. Now, open your jacket. And easy does it."

"What for?"

"You know what for."

"This ain't the time or place," Laurie said. There was a hesitation in his voice Jessica had never heard before.

"Do as I say," Heller said.

Slowly Laurie complied, revealing his brace of six-guns.

"Good, you're armed," the other said. "Figured you would be."

"You could always outdraw me. You know that."

"Yeah," Heller said. He held up the black-gloved claw that was his right hand. "That was my gun hand, remember? But now, who knows who's the faster draw? My left has had a lotta learning to do. Even so, I'll let you make the play."

"Can't we talk about this?"

Heller flexed the fingers of his left hand. "Time for talking was done a long time ago. Go for your iron."

Even from her side-on vantage point Jessica could see something new in Laurie's eyes. If she had to put a word on it, it was fear.

"I'm waiting," Heller said, the edge in his voice harder still. The two men were like that for several long moments, then . . .

"Hold it." A thumb clicked back a hammer and a gun on the end of a ramrod-straight arm had appeared from the doorway, slightly to the rear of Heller. It advanced until its muzzle gently rested against his skull. Rage erupted on Heller's face but his body remained still.

"Undo the gunbelt and let it fall,"

the man went on. As he came clearly into view Laurie saw a marshal's star on his chest.

His jaw muscles tightening up, Heller shucked his gunbelt so that it fell behind him.

The marshal picked it up and stepped off the boardwalk keeping his gun levelled. "Now over to the jailhouse yonder, nice and easy." As Heller stepped down, the marshal glanced at Laurie. "You too, mister. I wanna find out what this is all about."

Jessica grabbed Laurie's arm. "Oh, darling," she said, her voice shaking.

"Stay here," he said. "I don't want you mixed up in any bad business. I'll go over with the marshal, see what he wants. It shouldn't take long to sort this out. And don't worry, it's all over."

A gathering crowd watched the three men walk across the street.

"What was that all about?" the marshal asked Heller once they were behind closed doors in the law office.

"He knows," Heller grunted, his hooded eyes flicking at Laurie. "That's enough. This is between him and me and nobody else."

"Waal, two things I do know," the marshal said. "One is that you're wanted for robbing a local man last evening. Ben Whitehead came to town this morning to put in a report. Described you. Kinda unmistakable with that bum hand. Second thing I know, your name is Heller." He pointed to a wanted poster laid out on his desk. "That's you all right."

It was a recognizable facsimile of Heller, a little younger maybe, proclaiming his being wanted for bank robbery somewhere in Texas.

"Sure, that's me," Heller said. "But it's an old dodger. Check it out, pal, you'll find I served my time for that job."

"I'll check all right. Old Man Whitehead is still in town; I'll get him to make a positive identification of you as the man who robbed him.

You fit the description close enough as it is. Ain't many in town with a crook hand like that." With that he nodded to the back of the building and led the man away.

When Heller was behind bars, Laurie opened up his jacket and showed the marshal his own badge. "Laurie Bolan, Sheriff of Judgement Creek."

"So you're Bolan?" the marshal said, pleasure creasing his face as he extended his hand. "Glad to meet you, mister. Heard about you, of course. All this time and our trails have never crossed. Take a seat."

After a bout of warm hand-shaking both men sat and the marshal studied the wanted document. "Stroke of luck there," he said. "Old Man Whitehead comes into town to report a robbery and describes Heller. Neither my deputies or myself had seen the likes of him in the territory so I went through my dodger pile. Quite a stack. Once a varmint loses himself deep in Montana the law can never get him. Being where it is, Miles City acts as a focal point. Jumping off place for the trek west. Hunters in and out of the backwoods. We get all manner of folk up and down the river, good folk and trash alike."

He nodded to the document again. "Anyways, found this in my pile. Real old. But allus keeps my dodgers."

"Yeah, that's him," Laurie said, appraising the picture. "Regular owl-hoot in the old days. Looks like he ain't learned his lesson and is still riding bad trails."

"What's the story about you and him then?"

"Put him away, years ago. So long ago, plumb forgot about the varmint. Couldn't tell you how many years since I've seen him, then suddenly he's standing in front of me with a gun right here in Miles City. Looks like he still holds a grudge, fronting me like that. Tell you one thing: he's got a damn longer memory than I have!"

"Well, don't you worry none, Sheriff. Don't look like there'll be any problem identifying him for this local heist, then he'll be put away again. Territorial Penitentiary." He breathed deep. "What brings you to Miles, anyways?"

Laurie chuckled humourlessly. "Tenth wedding anniversary, would you believe. Came for a few days' holiday, some peace and quiet, and to look over your stores."

"Ah, that was your lady wife out there?"

"Yeah." Laurie looked down the corridor to the distant cell. "But being a law officer is a twenty-four hour job. Can't even have a couple of days' break without something cropping up."

"Huh, don't I know it, pal."

"I told the missus I wouldn't be longer than necessary," Laurie said, rising. "So if there's nothing else I'll get back to her."

"'Course. You do that. This business is nothing to do with you now. Unless you want me to lay a charge on him for behaviour likely to cause a breach of the peace. That'll add to his sentence. I can fix that, one lawman to another."

"Naw. Nothing came of it. I don't intend to press charges." He rose. "Good to have met you, Marshal."

"Same here, Laurie," the Miles man said, putting out his hand once more.

"You carry on having your holiday as if nothing had happened. And don't worry about that critter in there. With his record he ain't gonna be going no place for a long time."

6

JESSICA was close to the law office when he stepped out. "What was it, darling?" she said, taking his arm. "Such an ugly man. I could see hate all over his face."

"Guy called Heller. Anyway, he's out of harm's way. The marshal's got him for a robbery."

"A robbery?"

"Yeah. On the trail to town."

"I see. But why did he force himself on you? And another thing, you knew each other."

"Yeah. Listen, there's something I've gotta tell you." He looked up and down the street. "But I could sure use a whiskey or something. Let's talk over a drink."

They crossed to a saloon. "What'll you have?" he asked as he approached the bar.

"I think I'll try a bourbon. I've never had one, and it is our holiday."

"Fine. You sit down. I'll bring 'em over."

She sat at a table near a window and was looking through it when he rejoined her. She turned and looked at him. "So what is it?"

He threw his drink straight back. "You know I had a lotta jobs before coming to Judgement Creek?"

"Yes."

"Well, one of them was as a sheriff."

Her face changed. "A sheriff? You never told me."

"Naw. It was only a short spell. And it was years ago. Wasn't worth talking about."

"Where?"

"Back in Texas. Small town."

She sipped her drink and coughed. When she had recovered she asked, "And how does this Heller fit in?"

"While I was serving I had cause to put a few men in the slammer. You know, in the line of duty. Waal, he was one of them."

"How many years ago?"

"Oh, a dozen or more.

"And he comes after you *now*?"

"Seems like he's got a long memory and is still on the prod for me. It happens."

"He intended killing you, didn't he?"

"Let's forget about it. He's cooped up now. The local marshal has got him on a robbery charge."

"I've never been so frightened in my life."

"Yes, I could see you were shaken." He looked into her eyes, saw how disturbed she still was. "Listen, I think we'd better cut short our stay. You've got some new clothes. With the exception of this unfortunate incident we've had a good time. All we have to do is get something to take back for Johnny."

He looked out of the window, down the main drag towards the river, and chuckled humourlessly. "We've seen all Miles City has to offer anyways. Ain't the biggest place in the world."

"I think you're right, dear. And when we get back we'll say nothing to Johnny about this. We don't wish to upset him unduly." She took another sip, this time more cautiously. "It explains one thing."

"What's that?"

"The way you handled that roustabout who shot the sheriff a few years ago. You were the talk of the town for weeks. A storekeeper taking a hardcase into custody. Folks couldn't understand it."

"Well, when we get back ain't no need to tell 'em about me being a lawman once."

"Why not? It's nothing to be ashamed of, Laurie."

"All the same." He caught her looking at him and added, "I could do with another drink."

"Give me a moment to finish this one. Then I'll have another one, too."

A minute later he took her glass. "We'll have one more and get ourselves back to the hotel. Your clothes will have been delivered and I know you'd like to look at them again before we pack them up ready for the buggy. Then to bed early and we'll head out in the morning."

"What about your suit? The man said it'd be a couple of days before it was ready."

"Oh, yeah, I was forgetting. I'll get him to send it via the stage."

On the way back to the hotel he called in at the telegraph office to send a wire to Judgement Creek letting folks know they were returning early. But the machine was dead.

★ ★ ★

The damp morning air was like a knife. Their buggy laden with boxes, Laurie gigged the team and they started moving. As they rode past the river a light mist drifted above the water's surface, groping for the jetties of the waterfront. As fingers could grope from the past.

Once they were clear of the town, Jessica noted her husband look back, just once. As though saying goodbye to some element in his past life?

Or was he checking they weren't being followed? She was disturbed. She had never found him to have kept anything from her before. And what was so bad about having been a lawman before?

From the past, fingers groping.

7

IT was late morning when Stub-Tail Wilson rode into Judgement Creek. He was another in the bad-man business. With his face on a string of wanted posters, he was not the first of his kind to seek refuge in the lawless wilds of Montana. He had been on the lam for months and aimed to cover as much territory as he could each day, his plan being to get as far north as he could then to hide-out a spell. And today there was still riding light. For days now he had skirted towns but Judgement Creek was a natural bottleneck in the rocks and unavoidable for the traveller. Forced to ride through the place he hadn't intended stopping but as he rode along the main drag of the little settlement the aroma of good cooking assailed his nostrils. Days of jerky had tightened the belt around his already diminutive frame and put him in mind of a good meal. Hell, showing his face wouldn't do no harm, not out here in the middle of nowhere. He spied a livery stable advertising horse feed and he nudged his tired mount towards it.

He slipped out of the saddle, his slight build masked by the mackinaw he had bought way back in anticipation of the northern weather ahead.

Deaney was shoeing a horse when the little man came through the door. "Howdy, stranger," he said, giving a final scrape with his file and letting the shod hoof drop to the ground. "What can I do for you?"

"You can water and feed my hoss?"

"Sure thing. That's what I'm here for, feller."

The stranger passed the reins of his own mount to the ostler. "I smelled good cooking as I came down the street. There an eats-house hereabouts?"

Yeah, the finest. "Cross the street, down a block. Can't miss it. Run by a pal of mine, Roy. Roy the Boy we call him. English feller, but don't hold that against him. Best cook this side of the Missouri."

With an "Obliged," the newcomer left.

Meanwhile, in the saloon, Mayor Ade Newcomb dutch-shuffled a deck of cards. He ran a logging business at the end of the valley but always found time for a midday game of cards. He placed the straightened deck in front of him while, one by one, his regular partners joined him: Red, Pete, and a couple of storekeepers.

Max, the big German trapper took up the last seat. Now washed up and in his town clothes, he looked a different man. "The one thing I think of as I'm heading back to town out of the mountains is a drink and a game of cards."

The mayor unfastened his jacket, exposing his multi-coloured vest rounded out by a bulging stomach. "OK, then, let's see some action."

Over in the eats-house, Stub-Tail Wilson finished his meal and belched. As he fished through his pockets to pay the check it hit him that his funds were lower than he cottoned to. For months he'd been living on the proceeds of his last knock-over. It had been a lush haul and he still had mazuma left, so he wasn't broke. But he needed a sizable grubstake so that when it came time to hole-up he could buy himself a supply of chow for as long as it took.

Mulling over his financial situation, he made for the saloon. He ordered himself a rye and surveyed the occupants, checking first and foremost for the glint of a lawman's badge. None. Around a stove in the middle of the room a bunch of old cracker-barrel types were jawing away. In a corner a couple of mountain men in furs and overshoes.

He'd got a full belly of chow and by now his horse would be well fed. He'd have one drink and light a shuck. But something took his eye at the far end of the room. A card game. There was good money on the table and he could tell by the dress of the players that there was more where that came from.

His brain kicked the circumstances around. There were two things in life he could handle: a six-gun and a deck of cards. Mebbe this rough-edged saloon could be his means of working up a grubstake.

With these thoughts, he unbuttoned his mackinaw, bought another drink and watched the progress of the game. He bided his time until a convenient break, then sauntered over. "Hi, fellers," he said, keeping to the etiquette and staying his distance until welcomed.

The participants looked up, some nodded, some spoke.

"This a closed game," he went on, "or can any poke join in?"

"Just a friendly game between locals, mister," a red-haired fellow said.

"OK," he said, forcing a smile. "I understand." He knew better than to push himself in a strange town — it was common for locals not to invite strangers into their circle — so he strolled back to the bar. But on his return he located himself at the nearest point of the counter to the card table. There was still a chance he could get drawn in, and he knew it. He kept his back to the game, feigning disinterest and bought another drink.

A few deals later, two of the players made their excuses about work and other tasks, and withdrew. It was clearly a regular lunchtime game of fixed duration.

The departure left four at the table, around which a low-voiced conversation developed. Wilson knew what was going on. There is always one who wants to keep on playing; one with the bug and who is prepared to bend unwritten rules about letting strangers in. The listener deciphered one of the low voices. "You know we don't like outsiders in, Ade," he heard.

"Won't do any harm," came the reply. "Main game's over, anyhows."

Listening hard but giving the outward appearance of ignoring the interchange, Wilson bought another drink. A minute or so later a raised voice came to him over the smoky air of the saloon. "Still want a game, mister? Make it a fivesome?"

Wilson turned. The invitation was coming from a fat guy in a dude collar with black string tie and a fancy vest.

"Yeah, sure," Wilson said, picking up his glass and strolling over. He dropped his slight frame into a chair.

"Poker," the plump peacock said as he shuffled the cards. Tidying the deck he placed it on the table offering cuts for deal. As the others took their cards, the peacock introduced them. "Red, Pete, Max. And I'm Ade Newcomb."

"Name's Frank," Wilson said, giving them the first name he thought of. "Frank Slater."

For a spell the game moved slowly with small pots. Deliberately Wilson played carelessly, dropping pots to the others to keep them interested while

72

he weighed them up. The peacock was the most adventurous, the enjoyment he got from the game suggesting he was the one who had persuaded the others to let the stranger play. Of the others, Red was cautious in his style sometimes to the point of immobility. The one called Max played in a casual, bemused way while the fourth played a rational, take-it-or-leave-it game. All different styles of play but there was one thing they had in common. All four had money.

Progressively Wilson stepped up a gear, raising stakes and playing to win. He knew by their attire and the dismissive way they handled the larger stakes they were big guys, the kind of men who controlled the undercurrents of a town. But they didn't faze him. He'd met and handled bigger.

By the time he had a hundred dollars in front of him, the friendliness was disappearing from their voices. "Where you hail from, Frank?" the one called Red said as he dealt.

"Back aways," Wilson said, picking up his cards.

The redheaded one fanned his cards. "And where you headed?"

"Just riding through," Wilson said, rearranging his own hand.

Red didn't like the non-answers. He looked up from his cards and studied the newcomer. "Those ain't working hands. You ain't no farmer or trapper. And you ain't used to handling cattle." After a pause, he added, "There's only one reason I know of why a man without a visible trade buries himself in wild, rough country."

Wilson took note of the challenge but didn't react. He had a temper which could become uncontrollable, but for the moment he was thinking clear. Now antagonism was manifest the game had to end quickly. He could withdraw at the end of the present hand, but that wasn't his style. Not while these guys had still got thick billfolds in their wallet pockets. No, it was the time for the big play. It had to

74

be quick and that meant bending Lady Luck's arm. There was a high chance they wouldn't spot his tricks. Although they were big in their own backyard, it was a penny-ante town. These hicks had never pitted themselves against a man of his card-playing calibre. OK, if they did raise a ruckus . . . well, they'd never met a man who could handle himself like Wilson in those circumstances either.

It was his turn to deal and he shuffled the deck, but in such a way that he knew the disposition of critical cards. He surveyed the other four. Easy meat. "How about upping the stakes?" he suggested, still making a pretence at shuffling the pasteboards.

"What's on your mind?" Red asked.

"Five dollars a chip."

Red blew through his teeth. "A mite steep, ain't it?" .

"Come on, Red," the peacock said, the challenge bringing a gleam to his eye.

Eventually the others shrugged in

acquiescence, and Wilson dealt out five cards per man. On his left, Pete put up a five spot ante. To his left, Red put up the ten dollar straddle, then Wilson dealt.

Max, the next around the table, rearranged his hand. He had a pair of queens backed up by a small pair. Not brilliant, but enough on which to play, so he put up twenty dollars.

Last in the betting was Ade Newcomb. Three fives were enough to double the bet and he pushed out forty dollars.

Wilson picked up his five cards. The three high hearts he had planted nestled comfortably in his grip. He counted out forty dollars from his takings and pushed them to the middle.

The deciding passed from him to Pete who was thoughtfully weighing his cards. Hesitant to come into a doubled pot on two small pairs, he threw in.

That left the play to Red. Endowed with spades, four cards to a flush, he thought the gods were smiling, and added thirty dollars to the ten in front of him.

In between serving drinks Manny watched from behind the bar. It had been a long time since he'd seen such high-rolling.

"Cards?" Wilson asked to start the next phase of play.

"Yeah," Red said. "One." He kept his face impassive when he picked up another spade.

Max's new cards were no improvement, leaving him still with queens up.

Newcomb dispensed with the dross in his hand and picked up two nines, making a full house.

"Two," Wilson said, announcing his intention as dealer, then deftly slipped to himself the two hearts waiting for him at the bottom of the deck. "OK," he went on, confident that none of the backwoods bozos had seen his action. "New bets."

The German trapper checked, tapping the edge of his cards on the table.

Newcomb confidently doubled on his full house. Now sure of taking the suckers, Wilson doubled. Momentarily Red considered his ace high flush. "See yuh," he said, pushing out another forty.

Max grunted and threw in his hand, abandoning his stake. Wilson nodded and Red showed his five cards. But that, and Newcomb's full house, paled against the dealer's exposed royal straight flush. "Tough luck," Wilson said, leaning forward. Slowly he pulled the pot towards him, netting a take a little shy of two Cs. He could have stopped at that point, he had intended to as he had ample now for supplies. But these bozos were easy meat and he was enjoying himself. Not a card-player amongst them, not one who knew the business.

He placed the deck in the now bare middle of the table. "New hand, gentlemen?" He would sure play some more if the suckers were willing.

Red made a show of counting the

bills remaining in his wallet. "No, that's enough for me, boys. I got things to do." Then he added in a disgruntled tone, "Less expensive things."

"Enough for me too," Max said and finished the dregs from his glass. "I ain't spent a month trapping at the end of nowhere to lose the haul in a couple of pasteboard rounds."

Newcomb was looking hard at Wilson. "It's enough for me, too. But I ain't referring to losing a bundle. Money's money, goes and comes. What I've had enough of is playing with a card sharp."

"Card sharp?" Pete queried as he buttoned up his jacket in preparation to leave.

"Yeah," Newcomb went on. "This panhandler slipped himself some goodies off the bottom of the deck."

"I didn't see him playing crook," Pete said.

Newcomb grunted cynically. "You guys weren't quick enough to see. Like me, you ain't used to fancy play. But I see'd it. This long rider is nothing but a damn card-shifter."

"You're gonna have to take that back, mister," Wilson said, things beginning to well up inside him over which he had no control. He pocketed his pickings, then stood up. You take that back," he said in a hard tone, "or you back it up."

"*Mein herr*," Max said, rising. "You are talking to the mayor of our town."

Behind the bar, Manny's usual smiling face had become serious.

"I don't care if he works in the White House," Wilson hissed. "He takes his mean-mouthing back."

"Like hell I will," Newcomb replied, standing.

Wilson was going over the edge. He couldn't take instruction or reprimand which was why he had never been able to hold down a legitimate job in his life. "You got one more chance, fancy vest," he said, backing a step.

Newcomb was firm. "Put that money back on the table, you no-good, cheating drifter."

As he spoke he moved forward to tap the table in emphasis. But his plump hand didn't get to the table. The movement alone was enough to trigger the tension that had built up in Wilson. Out came both guns, firing at the level. Slugs cratered Newcomb's chest, slamming him backwards.

To Wilson's left Manny came up from behind his counter with a shot-gun but Wilson half-glanced and triggered something his way. The bartender crashed backwards and disappeared behind the bar.

"Anybody else?" Wilson said, backing so that he could cover all the occupants. By this time every man in the place, mountain men, herdsmen, was on his feet but none of them dared move.

Wilson continued his backward movement until he was at the door. "Right then, don't any assholes follow me." He slipped one gun into its holster and opened the door with his free hand.

Then he was gone.

Red leapt behind the bar and knelt down to turn over the unfortunate bartender who was lying face down in an awkward contortion of limbs. The woollen hat was flat on the floor. It was the first time Red had seen the bearded Jew bare-headed. And there was an ugly, black hole in his forehead. Red stood up. "Manny's poured his last drink, guys."

"I'll get the doc for Adey," one of the old-timers said, as the clatter of Wilson's boots on the boardwalk began to fade.

"Hold your hosses," another said. "That varmint ain't joshing. Reckon he means what he says about blasting anybody who puts his face outside yet awhile."

"Figured him for a four-flusher," Red said, coming slowly from behind the bar. "Them hands of his. Like a woman's."

"No need for the doctor here either, *mein herr*," Max said, now on his knees by the side of the mayor's corpse. He rose. "Get the sheriff."

Pale and shaking, Pete dropped into a chair. "We told you, Max, Sheriffs outa town."

8

LAURIE BOLAN and his wife rolled leisurely in their buggy towards Judgement Creek. Although the rigour of the climate was losing its bite, the trail earth still retained its hardness so the going was easy. To their north the slopes rose, the green of the trees shading into white towards the craggy peaks.

As they travelled they spoke little of the incident in Miles City. It had clearly shaken Laurie at the time but it was behind them now and, at least for the present and near future, the man called Heller was going noplace and causing nobody trouble.

From the time they cleared the settlement, she had been aware of her husband undergoing a change. As the miles stacked up, piling distance between the buggy and the town he gradually returned to the Laurie she knew. Some burden under which he had been crumpling seemed to slip from his shoulders.

They were still some distance from their destination when Laurie spotted a rider on the trail ahead. The man was approaching at a dead run.

"He's heading outa Judgement Creek," Laurie observed when the shape became more distinct, "but I don't recognize him." As the lawman he not only made it his business to know everybody in town but also the trappers and the other regular visitors. "Pushing his hoss mighty hard too," he noted, "for a stranger just riding through."

He kept his eyes on the rider who suddenly stopped his pinto and looked their way. After a brief pause the man turned his mount off the trail to head north through a break in the trees.

"I wish the feller had got within hailing distance," Laurie commented. "If he's a stranger in the territory I'd have told him there ain't nothing that way'cepting rough rock country and grizzlies."

When they reached the gap in the trees through which the rider had gone, Laurie checked the harnessed horse and pulled in the buggy. He could still make out the man in the distance, now making heavy going of the grade. "Ain't a big guy. Could be a youngster. For his sake, sure hope he's equipped for bad weather. It ain't gonna feel like spring up in the mountains yet awhile."

"Did he veer off the trail because he saw us?" Jessica pondered. "Or was it a coincidence?"

"Dunno, Jessy. But there's something funny. Out in the wilds where you can go for a week without seeing anybody, a man usually stays around long enough to say howdy."

He gigged the horse onward and dismissed the encounter from his mind as he anticipated their arrival in town and the pleasure of seeing little Johnny again.

When they did hit town Laurie could see something was wrong. There were more horses than usual on the hitchrail outside the law office and a crowd on the boardwalk.

Norman, his young deputy, stepped down to the street and approached as Laurie whoa'ed the horse. "Thought you wouldn't be back for another coupla days, Laurie," he said.

"We'd had our fill," the lawman said, pulling on the brake.

"Anyways, sure glad to see yuh. We got a problem."

Laurie looked at the serious faces of the men that were joining the deputy around the buggy. There was Pete, Max, Red and others. "What's the pitch?" the sheriff wanted to know.

"Mayor's been killed, Laurie."

"Adey? Dead? How?"

"Drifter shot him up over a card game. Got Manny behind the bar too."

The lawman absorbed the news. "You got the varmint?"

"No. He got the drop on everybody in the saloon and headed outa town."

"How long since?"

"An hour."

"You've wired territorial capital?"

"Nah, line's dead."

"Well, we're gonna have to handle this by ourselves until the authorities can be notified."

"It's been longer than an hour since the jasper hit the trail, *mein herr*," Max put in. "More like two."

Laurie looked at Norman. The young man was poor material for a deputy, no organizer of men and dodged gun-play when he could. But nobody else wanted the job. "Two hours and you ain't out after him yet, Norman?"

"I was just getting up a posse," the deputy explained.

"OK, how many men you got?"

"Three."

"Then let's ride."

Red raised his hand. "Hold back there, Laurie. We'll need more than that. Now he's killed a couple of guys he won't hesitate to make targets outa anybody on his trail."

"Are we men or mice?" Laurie snapped.

"Red is right," Pete added. "The feller's an undersized runt but he's gun-wise."

Laurie pondered on the words. "Undersized, you say? Short feller, in a mackinaw?"

"Yeah."

"And riding a pinto?"

"That's right," Deaney said. "He stabled the hoss with me for a spell."

"Seen the critter," Laurie said. "Pulled off the trail ahead of me and the missus some miles outa town. Heading north over rough country now."

He looked back at his deputy. "Who've you got to ride with you?"

"Red, Pete and Max."

"And we're gonna string the jasper up," Pete said, "if we don't gun him down first. Ain't a man here who didn't think Adey was the best of guys. And poor Manny never did nobody no harm in his whole life."

"There ain't gonna be no lynchings while I'm around," Laurie said. "Not like before. We're gonna do this proper and legal this time."

He surveyed the crowd. "You men, we got a job to do. We need three more." He pointed at men he knew capable. "You — Miff, Spud, Deaney. You got what it takes. How about it?"

The three were amenable, having more faith in him than his deputy.

"OK," he said, having ascertained the extra three were willing to take his instruction, "get yourselves each a good horse, guns and ammo. Extra clothing too. It can be cold out there."

He took out his timepiece. "I'll see yuh all here, no longer than twenty minutes. We still got a lotta daylight left." He looked at Red, Pete and Max. "You were there at the shooting. While the others are saddling up, you go with Norman to the law office and look through the dodgers. It'll be a help to know if this guy is on any wanted lists."

He turned to his wife. "Jessy, take the buggy and say hello to little Johnny for me. Tell him how I'm tied up with legal business. He'll understand."

She touched his arm as he made to descend. "Be careful, Laurie."

★ ★ ★

In the prescribed time there were eight riders mounted outside the law office. Laurie had a wanted poster in his hand which he was displaying to the others. A perusal of the files by the witnesses had turned up a likeness to the man. A short-ass renegade, known as Stub-Tail Wilson, wanted for murder and bank robbery in Oklahoma.

"This is the varmint," he said, making sure everyone had seen the paper. Then he folded it up and put it into his pocket. "It's up to us to make him rue the day he rode into Judgement Creek. Let's ride."

9

SHERIFF BOLAN halted his posse at the break in the trees where earlier in the day he'd seen their quarry cut off the trail and into the trees. He trained his eyes on the fingers of snow feeling their way down the slope. Some way up the whiteness was disturbed. He looked beyond to the rocky tree-covered masses to the north, then turned in his saddle and spoke to the men behind him.

"Listen up, men. This is it. You can see where the varmint has gone. I don't have to tell you what the terrain is like up there. The chinook is bringing spring to the low country, but up there they haven't heard what spring is yet. There'll be snow, winter cold, and the country is dog-rough. Anybody wants to turn back, he'd best say so now."

"We're with you, *mein herr*," Max

said. The sentiment was echoed around the gathering.

"OK," Laurie said, and he hauled on the reins heading his mount up the slope. The others followed in single file.

A half-mile on they had to dismount and proceed on foot. Then the grade steepened further and Laurie could hear grumblings amongst the men. "If that Wilson can do it, so can we," he shouted back by way of encouragement.

Another half-mile on, Spud's horse lost its footing, scrabbled and fell. Laurie turned to see its owner helping it to its feet. By the time the unhappy creature was standing it could be seen to have a limp. "Pulled a muscle, Laurie," Spud said, examining the leg. "Can't go on. She's a good hoss. I ain't shooting her."

"Understand your feelings, Spud," the lawman said. "Look, it's gonna be dark soon. You're gonna have a helluva problem getting a lame hoss back. Nothing for it but for you to head back now." He sighed deep. "Figure one of the men had better go with you. Miff, you and he's pals. You'd better go."

Miff nodded. "OK, Sheriff."

The party split, they made their goodbyes and the six resumed their trek up the slopes. A half-mile further the terrain levelled enough for them to ride, but a short distance on and they had to dismount yet again in the face of rising ground and a turn in the weather. Snow moted down, softly, gently, covering everything in white dust like someone was beating a carpet somewheres up in heaven.

With rising elevation the wind grew teeth.

"Hold on there, Laurie," Red shouted, straggling behind after a hard haul up a particularly sharp grade. The column came to a standstill. "This ain't no use," the man went on. "Light's fading fast. This weather gets worse, we're gonna have a problem simply surviving, never mind catching the owlhoot."

"Red's right, Laurie," Norman said.

In the lead Max stopped in his ascent and turned, his one eye spearing his youngster. Ach, he didn't expect anything better from the sheriffs weak-willed deputy.

"Yeah," Laurie agreed. "Ain't much point in this weather. What do the rest of you men think?"

By his demeanour it was clear that turning back was not amongst Max's options. In his furs and with his scowling face he looked like some ornery grizzly as the remainder voiced their general agreement that they were on a hiding to nothing.

"*Gott in Himmel*," the German snapped. "With the telegraph wires down, we are the only ones who can do anything about getting Adey's killer. You bozos want the varmint to get clean away?"

"That ain't the point any more," Red said. "We've done what we could."

"There's something in what he says,

you know, Max," Laurie added.

"*Nein*. There is nothing in what he says. You are sheriff. If nobody else, you should continue the pursuit of justice."

Laurie remained indecisively silent.

"The hell with all of you," the trapper grunted. "Then I will carry on alone."

Laurie watched the German resume his struggle up the slope, pulling his saddle and pack horses. "Ain't right I leave him by himself. After all, it is law work. I suppose if anyone's going with him it'll have to be me. Norm, you go back to town and look after the office in my stead. I'll keep up with Max. He's a trapper and knows how to handle himself out here. The other three go back with Norman. You should be able to catch up with Spud and Miff. They ain't gonna be making good time with a lame hoss."

The listeners nodded, not unhappy to be out of it.

"In the morning, Norman," the

lawman went on, "you do your damnedest to locate the fault on the line. We gotta let the authorities know what's happened here. Especially try to get word to Fort Peck. That looks like the way Wilson's headed." He pointed down the column. "We'll take the pack horse," he continued. "I want whatever food you've got. This is gonna be a bigger job than I expected."

Max had paused at the new development on his backtrail and was looking down. "Make sure there's a couple of tarps aboard," he shouted back. "And we'll want a few extra blankets from you fellers."

Again goodbyes were made and the two men pressed upwards while the four others began the descent through the trees.

With darkness the snow worsened, the temperature dropped. "We better look for a good spot to camp," Laurie said. "Ain't no sense in carrying on. Let's look for an overhang for shelter."

His companion stopped and quartered

their surroundings. "Better than that," he suggested, waving an arm westward. "We work our way half a mile west; across the ridge there's a trapper's cabin. It's out of our way but we'll have a good night's rest. That's more than Wilson will be getting. A rest such as afforded by that will give us an edge come morning."

Despite the darkness Max knew the way and they made the cabin in good time. The place was long since deserted but in serviceable condition. In no time they had themselves sealed against the elements with a welcome fire.

"Good job for us you knew of this place," Laurie said after they'd taken a bite to eat and were relaxing in the firelight, the sheriff with his thoughts and Max puffing on a cherrywood. "You sure know your terrain."

"Been here all my growed-up life, *mein herr*. Came over from the old country when I was still a young man. Come from a military family. Joined the Second Cavalry in Montana chasing

Indians. That's how come I lost my eye. Spot of trouble with some piegans hell-bent on horse-stealing raids. Got hit with one of the varmint's war clubs. Huh, you know what it was made of? A white man's wagon spoke."

He chuckled as though it were a joke. "That's what we've taught 'em: how to make clubs out of wagon wheels. Well, then Uncle Sam says there was no place in his army for a one-eyed Kraut, so I was discharged. I wasn't going back to Europe and I needed to do something to support myself but I didn't know what. During my duty at the forts I'd seen all kinds of trappers and hunters. I suppose I'd always envied them, so I became one. Spent all my time since, combing Yellowstone and Musselshell country. Ain't been a bad life."

Neither spoke for a while then Max broke the silence with, "You're doing the right thing here, Sheriff. We can't let the renegade go."

"Yeah, but we gotta take care with

him. He's got a track record. This ain't the first time he's had the law after him."

"There's two of us."

"Yes, but he's an experienced man with his hardware. You might be OK but I'm no pistolero. Never claimed to be."

"Don't worry, Sheriff. Like I says, we got the edge on him. He don't know we're still after him. He'll think anybody following will have thrown in the towel when the weather turned. We work it right, we should be able to get the drop on him." He winked his one eye. "Just like you did on that bozo in the saloon a few years back."

Laurie remained silent, looking at the flames.

10

HELLER had only broken out of the slammer once before, and that was a long time ago, when he was a young roustabout. But he needed to break out of this one. If he could do it at all, it would be out of a one-hoss place like Miles City. It stuck in his craw that, after ten years, he'd finally located the man they called the Prince and, just when he'd got the bozo at the business end of his Colt, he'd got stymied by some no-account lawman. His own fault. If he'd put a slug in that old critter out on the trail, he wouldn't be here now.

He looked around the cell. Cramped, a small barred window, two bunks, a blanket, a bucket. Not much promise. But he noted that the means of access was a narrow barred door set in a brick wall, and not a grid spanning the width of the cell. To his experienced eye that circumstance had potential. It gave blind spots. A man on the outside of the door couldn't see the adjacent sides of the interior. The unseen parts were narrow. How could he take advantage of that? Obviously it was naive to think he could jump the lawman; but there had to be a way he could make use of the small amount of cover.

He sat on one of the palliasses, looked, listened, thought. Out front there were two lawmen, the marshal and his deputy. They had stopped talking. Heller wondered what their routine was. Then he heard the marshal speak. "I'll take the night shift. It's got all the makings of a quiet spell. You may as well git on home."

There was movement and clattering, then goodnights were exchanged. The outer door opened and closed, and the marshal was alone. After a moment, Heller heard feet and the lawman's face was peering through the bars. Heller had already noticed that the man made regular checks. The prisoner didn't move under the scrutiny and the marshal returned to the front office.

Heller mulled over the possibilities. And it wasn't long before he had an idea. For a start he needed cord, something like that. Then he observed that the palliasse on which he lay was stitched together with twine. That might serve his purpose; but there was nothing he could do while the marshal made his regular checks on the cell and its occupant.

With the passage of time came darkness and a fall in temperature. Heller had wrapped the blanket around him and was lying still. The lamps from the front office cast shadows of the bars on the floor. After an hour or so the lawman broke his pattern, became complacent and ceased coming to the barred door. Heller eased himself off the bunk and crept across the cell to look through the door. The man was sitting with his feet on his desk engrossed in some book.

Heller returned to his bunk and set to work, quietly picking at the stitching of the palliasse. Eventually he had a serviceable length.

That was the first step in his plan but he still needed a couple of breaks. Everything comes to he that waits, he mused as he lay back on the bunk. Sure enough the first break came some time later when he heard the marshal get up and open the outer door. When he heard the door close, Heller rose and looked from the cell. The man had gone outside, sounded like he was checking the horses or something. Heller moved quickly and as quietly as he could. The man was only absent for mere minutes but it was long enough for his purposes.

With that phase over, he needed a second break. That came when he heard the lawman clanking a coffee pot.

He went again to the cell door. "Say, mister," he said. "It's real cold back here. You got another blanket or something? And I'd sure appreciate a cup of hot coffee."

The marshal looked up from his task. "OK."

A few minutes later the lawman was standing at the cell door, blanket over one arm and a tin mug in the other. He studied the gaps in the grid for a second. "I could pass the blanket through the bars," he said, "but I'm gonna have to open the door to bring the coffee in. Now listen up. I'm doing you a favour here so I don't want no trouble. You lean on the outer wall with your back to me."

Heller got off the bunk, moved to the far end of the cell and leant on the wall as instructed.

"Legs well apart," the marshal went on, without moving.

Again Heller followed instructions. The marshal looked at him for another moment, satisfying himself there was nothing his prisoner could do without giving the lawman a chance to do something about it. What the hell could a one-armed man do anyway?

He lowered the mug to the floor and with the blanket still over his arm, he slipped the key into the lock. But, as he pushed open the door, he was startled by the harsh sound of scraping to his left. Before he could react something large slammed against him.

In the semi-darkness, with his attention wholly on the renegade, he hadn't noticed the absence of one of the bunks. That oversight was what Heller had been banking on when he had positioned the wooden frame against the wall; leaning it so precariously that the slightest pull on the twine connecting the top of the upended bunk to the door would bring its heavy weight crashing down.

Before the unfortunate lawman could recover, Heller had leapt across the cell and was slamming him in the head with his one capable fist. He continued the blows until the man was unconscious.

For a second Heller looked at the prone man. When he came to he would no doubt round up a posse. But the prisoner wasn't too concerned. The ground outside was hard and, as long as he wasn't seen making his getaway, they would find it difficult to pick up his trail. OK, he could still get captured. It was a chance, he knew that. But the way he felt at the moment he didn't really care whether he got caught — just as long as he had time to finish the task he'd set himself.

★ ★ ★

Heller was cold. The night wind had a bite to it and was bringing a fall of snow. Not heavy, but enough to bleach his eyebrows and chin bristles. He'd ridden without a sense of time. Was it midnight? Could be; couldn't tell. The horse was tired and he knew he was. He reined in and tried to make sense of his surroundings. Wherever he was, he was still some distance from Judgement Creek.

Through the white veil he could see a faint glimmer. Some kind of habitation. Now he was in the vicinity he wasn't keen to be seen but both he and the animal could benefit from shelter, so he nudged his mount in the direction of the light. Eventually he could make out a cabin lodged in the lee-side of the rocks. As he neared and could make out details he could see a lean-to. Under these conditions it would be possible for him to avail himself of the facility and light out in the morning, with no one the wiser. City folk didn't realize a wind-break in the right position can be as good as four walls. He smiled to himself when he got there and saw it harboured a store of winter hay. Huh, who wants a first-class hotel?

He got his horse under cover, tethered it within access to the feed and unsaddled it. Then he relocated some more of the stuff to make a bed for himself. Within minutes he was sleeping.

It was the kicking of his boot-sole that woke him. He didn't know how long he had been asleep. Though the roused man was not yet in control of his faculties his hand went instinctively to his gun butt.

"Let that be, stranger." The voice, a female's, came from a shape in the darkness. Even though the voice was feeble, what made him heed the instruction was the ominous silhouette of a shot-gun.

His hand fell back. "Just sheltering, ma'am."

"Why didn't you knock the goddamn door?"

"Didn't want to disturb nobody, ma'am. Seeing's it was late and all."

The shot-gun lowered. "You can't mean no trouble. Otherwise you'd have caused it by now. Come on inside, feller. It's warmer. Your hoss will be OK here."

It was plain the toil of many years weighed heavily on her as she slowly moved her bulk towards the cabin.

"Might as well know, mister," she went on when they were inside, "I live by myself."

The light of the oil-lamp showed her face to be puffy, her eyes marbles deeply set in dough. Somewhere between fifty and sixty now, it was unlikely she had ever been attractive. But she had the buxom roundness of a mother hen and there was a friendly twinkle in her eye. "Ain't got nothing worth stealing. And if you got any other intentions, there's zilch I can do about it. And I'm old enough not to'

"Nothing to fear, ma'am. Just wanna shut my eyes."

"There's coffee, bread, cheese. When you've done, a bunk of furs. Ain't nothing warmer than a heap of furs. Help yourself." She picked up a pipe and put a taper to it from the fire. "Kids have grown up and gone." She pointed to a framed photograph on the wall. "Old man passed on a couple of years back. That's his mound outside. You might have stumbled on it in the dark. I'll put some flowers on it again when the spring blooms come out."

"Me, ain't got no wife or kids. Just a hoss."

She lit the pipe and puffed. "Keeps myself to myself and don't ask no questions of strangers." She watched a cloud of smoke rise. "Folks down at Judgement Creek call me a passel of things but my given name's Kathy."

Mention of the town interested him. "So we ain't far from Judgement Creek?"

"Half a dozen miles down the valley."

He nodded. After a spell he said, "Name's Luke."

★ ★ ★

Come morning the lady Kathy served him a hot plate of hash. She went about her chores while he went to the lean-to and saddled up his horse. As he mounted up, she came outside. "Enjoyed your company, stranger."

"I didn't do nothing or say nothing," he said.

"Still enjoyed your company."

He looked down the valley. In daylight he recognized the trail to Judgement Creek. On the far side in the distance he saw what looked like a man-made break in the trees. "What's that, ma'am?"

"The trail up to the old Columbia mine. They managed to get some ore out of her for a spell but it's been derelict for years."

He gripped the rein in preparation for departure. "Obliged for the hospitality, ma'am. Be seeing yuh."

"Any time, feller."

He pushed the gelding down the slope. Hitting the trail, he turned in the saddle. The woman was still looking at him. He waved once and urged his horse to a canter.

11

LAURIE woke to the smell of meat being cooked. He rolled over and saw the carcass of a rabbit on a spit over the fire. "Hell of an advantage being out here with a trapper," he observed as he hauled himself into a sitting position and looked at his companion busying himself at a ramshackle table.

"Up at dawn," Max said. "Didn't take long to catch myself a little critter."

"Why didn't you wake me?"

"*Nein*, a man sleeps hard like you did, he needs his shut-eye. Coffee?"

"Coffee, too! Like some swank hotel here."

He hauled himself to his feet and joined his companion at the stove, gratefully putting his hands around the proffered mug.

The German nodded at the grimy window. "Snow's stopped."

Laurie remembered their task and his early-morning euphoria waned. "Damn snow. Bad luck that. Cover his tracks."

"There is advantage, *mein herr*. The varmint will make new tracks."

Laurie grunted. "This is big territory, Max. Be like a long odds crap game stumbling over his trail."

"Ain't as bad as you make out, Laurie. Looks like he's headed north. Fort Peck, Canada, mebbe. If he keeps that course he'll find there's only one way through from this direction. Three Squaws Pass. That'll tie him down some."

The snow kept off and by noon they were crunching pine needles underfoot in big tree country. Red cedar, Douglas fir, spruce, reached to the sky to block out the sunlight. Attaining a ridge they took a rest on the apex.

Cold and unmotivated, Laurie leant heavily against the trunk of a fir and looked ahead. Beyond a shallow dip, nothing but more mountains. "Ain't nothing stopping him getting clean away to Canada," he said.

"There you go again," Max said, clearing some snow from a low rock and sitting on it. "To one who does not know it, this country looks big. It is big, huge, but the means of travel that it allows are limited. This, what's his name, Wilson, will not know the land. I do. Like water swirling round a funnel, the man will meander around, wasting time and energy, but will inevitably be channelled to one point. All we have to do is get some sign of which of the few points it's going to be. Have faith, *mein herr.*"

They crossed the ridge and dropped into the shallow valley. They were part way up the other side when Max raised his hand to stop his companion. Following the direction of the trapper's pointed finger, Laurie could see the reason for the halt. Some distance ahead were Indians in single file crossing their path.

"Let's get outa here," he said, yanking on his horse's hackamore. But when he turned he could see more Indians through the trees below them. In his panic he drew the Winchester from his saddleboot but Max's eye caught the movement. "Put it away, *mein herr*. It is best not to begin a meeting with a threat. Besides there are too many."

The Indians above had seen them. They stopped and looked down the slope. Max dropped his horse's rein. "Stay here and look after my mount," the trapper said. "The redman has only fear and mistrust of white men." And he started to climb up to the party.

As the lawman watched the progress of his companion Indians below and around him broke cover and began to approach in silence. Nervous, his face as white as the surrounding snow, he was aware of them making examination of the horses, running their hands over the animals.

When the German reached the

Indians there was some gesturing and, on the wind, Laurie caught snatches of some strange tongue. After a while his companion returned and began unbuckling a saddlebag, taking out a whiskey bottle and packs of tobacco. "Always have merchandise ready for trade," he said. He handed the goods to one of the nearby Indians, exchanging words in the tongue. He untied a blanket, held it high and shouted something to the leader who waved in acknowledgement.

"Might as well give them a blanket for good measure," he said to Laurie as he handed that item to one of the warriors. More words were exchanged and the redmen around them began to climb ahead.

"What are we trading for?" Laurie whispered.

"Information," the trapper said, then added with a chuckle, "and maybe our lives. Stay here until they've passed."

"You know their language."

"*Ja*. A dialect of Pend d'Oreille."

"You say they mistrust white men. You're white."

Max watched the natives making their ascent. "You know your ancient history? The old Greek states were always at war with each other, hated each other's guts. Kill any strangers on sight. But there were a few privileged individuals, belonging to no nation, who sailed the high seas and travelled unharmed between states, trading, passing messages. Such a man was known as χenos, meaning guest-friend. And he could only be such by operating alone. Obviously any strangers in large numbers constitute a threat. The Indians see me something like that."

"You know those redmen up there?"

"*Nein*. But they've heard of me."

"What's your secret?"

The trapper waved a farewell to the Indians above them as they began to move into the trees, resuming their trek. "Got no secret," he said. "The Indian is one of God's creatures and is entitled to live and have a square deal. You treat him that way he gives you a square deal."

"So what information did we trade for?"

"They seen a whitey earlier today, travelling north. Too distant to cross trails. But seems to fit the description of our man."

"They've told you where he is?"

"Better than that. They've told me how we can head him off."

The Indians had now disappeared. "Come on, *mein herr*," the trapper said. "As you Texans say, let's hit the trail. On the basis of what the Pend d'Oreille said, first chance we get we turn east."

Some miles ahead they changed course and for hours they worked upwards through forest and scrub until they hit a particularly dense patch. Time and time again the dispirited Laurie felt the urge to call a halt, make it plain to the bone-headed German that, despite the meagre information the natives had given, the chance of catching the renegade was diminishing fast. But he knew it would be no good. The trapper would insist on pressing on, and he would feel obliged to continue with him.

Eventually the trees thinned and a clearing could be seen ahead. Max paused before completely breaking cover and put out a fiat hand to stop his companion. He scrutinized the open space, then pointed. "*Himmel*. The Pend d'Oreille were right. Looks like the jasper went that way." His eagle eye had spotted tracks coming out of the forest some distance from their position.

Laurie squinted. "Hell, the things you see with one eye! I got two and I can't see anything."

"You wouldn't find it so bad, having one eye, *mein herr*. You only got one mouth but you're happy with that, are you not?" He beckoned. "Come."

They changed their course and worked their way to the disturbed snow.

"One man, one horse," the trapper said, after a second's contemplation.

"Could be anybody."

"No. The redmen only seen one man for days. "Sides, ain't many fool enough to bring a horse this high into the mountains. That's him all right." His eye followed the tracks. "The way I figure it, the route that bozo has chosen for himself means he's gonna hit d'Oreille Bluff."

He waved his arm in a north-easterly direction. "It's impassable at that point. When he hits the rock his choices will be very limited. He can backtrack down again. He won't do that; he's come this far already. What he'll do is figure out the lie of the rock, then aim to work his way upwards along its base until he gets to the ridge. From there he can get through at Three Squaws Pass. The point is, that course of action will bring him further this way. Do not worry, *mein herr*. Despite his lead on us we should be able to cut him off if we swing across and head for the Pass direct from here. Remember the water and the funnel."

A look of satisfaction came to Laurie's face. "Just hope we're in luck, pardner."

12

LIGHT snow began to fall again as the two men crossed the clearing into the trees heading for Three Squaws Pass. Above them the two sides of the pass reared, towering three hundred feet in the clear light. To their side the icy water of a creek swished through the rocks. Behind them their horses' hooves stuttered on the steepening grade. Max stopped and examined the way ahead. Steeper still.

"This is a crazy place for a horse," he said. He led his buckskin towards a cedar, indicating for Laurie to do likewise. "We're gonna have to make the rest without the animals."

They tethered their mounts to the tree and took their long weapons from the saddleboots. They thumbed in loads and continued the climb, the escarpments looming more and more ominously as they progressed. By the time they had attained the base from whence the massive rock thrust towards the heavens the snowfall had ceased. Before they emerged from the trees Max halted and pointed. The light fall of snow across the floor of the narrow pass was virginal.

"Nobody's been this way for a spell," he said.

"What now?"

"We wait a piece." He nodded along the foot of the rock. "If he's coming, that's the way it'll be."

They huddled behind the trees, pulling up their collars against the wind coming through the pass. A good half-hour passed and the cold was beginning to bite deep. Suddenly Max raised a gloved finger to indicate he had heard a sound, a faint sound, coming from the expected direction. So faint, Laurie couldn't hear it.

Eventually their straining ears could make out the definite crunch of gravel;

then a figure, small-framed, battered hat pulled low against the wind, trudging along the rock wall, leading a horse. Silently the two men removed the gloves from their trigger hands.

"Him?" Laurie whispered.

Max worked his shoulders in a 'can't tell' gesture. Then, as the walker neared, Max nodded very positively. With readied guns they waited till their quarry was into the turn of the rock.

"Hold it there, Wilson!" Laurie shouted. "We got you dead to rights."

The man froze. He couldn't go for his weapons: his mackinaw sealed up his handguns and his rifle was in the saddleboot.

"Wilson?" he yelled. "That ain't my name, stranger."

Laurie ignored the denial. "Leave go your hoss and walk steady this way," he went on. "This is the law. Sheriff of Judgement Creek with a posse."

Wilson squinted until he could make them out. "Judgement Creek? Ain't never heard of the place."

"Like hell you ain't."

"What do you want with me, Sheriff? I'm just a peaceable man making a peaceable journey."

"This ain't the place to argify. Start walking this way with your hands up."

The man in the mackinaw worked out the odds. He knew where his adversaries were and, despite what the man had shouted, he figured he was bluffing and that there were no more than two. He had nothing to lose. What was more, he had skill. He whirled backwards, flipping the Winchester out of the boot and dropping behind his horse, all in one balletic movement. Both the men's guns erupted and Wilson's horse dropped to its knees taking both charges. The fallen animal's rump remained high providing Wilson with cover from which he loosed off a couple of shots.

Laurie and his companion ducked back behind the trunks as bark splintered. Max tried for another shot but withdrew before a chunk of tree disintegrated close to where his head had been.

They stayed that way for a moment, then Max shouted, "Come on, Laurie. He's exposed on the side. We can take him from there." With that the burly trapper threw himself forward, his back landing hard against the next tree as Wilson's gun barked again and a bullet hit the empty air between the trees.

Laurie froze as Max sprang for another tree, firing on the way.

"For crissakes, follow me," Max yelled back. "What's the matter with you? I've told you: we work our way round, he'll have no cover."

Laurie appeared momentarily and triggered a couple of shots blind and wild in Wilson's direction. He made to move but a bullet fountained snow close to his feet and he fell back, his breath coming hard and freezing on the cold air.

Max glanced back at the stone-like lawman before diving for another tree. But this time a shot from Wilson caught the running man and sent him sprawling in the snow. Laurie watched him elbow to cover and collapse against the tree bole.

Above Max's faint groaning he could hear Wilson's agonized horse snuffling pathetically in its death throes. He chanced a look and saw the rump of the harrowed horse keel over.

Suddenly exposed, Wilson made a dash. Laurie raised his gun to his eye and fired. The renegade juddered and fell.

For a second Laurie couldn't understand why the man was still capable of trying to get up and make a run for it. The lawman moved forward nervously, firing a round ahead of the scrabbling man. Reaching him he stood over him before he could rise further. "You move one inch and you're blasted to hell," he said falteringly.

As he spoke he could see what had happened. The stock of the renegade's Winchester had taken the full force of his slug. The jasper had the luck of the devil himself. Laurie didn't know whether he was relieved or disappointed at the man's well-being.

Gripping his arm, the fallen Max watched the lawman, suddenly tough now the man was at his mercy. Laurie kept the rifle aimed with one hand while he used the other to take out the handcuffs from his pocket. But as he moved slowly forward he became aware he was bringing himself in range of the gunman's feet.

"Put your hands out for the cuffs," he said. "And don't think of kicking out; this gun blows your head away at the first sign. I ain't got no qualms, mister. You've already killed two of my pals and downed another."

"Not me, mister. I'm sorry about your pardner over there. I was only defending myself. But I ain't done no killing."

"There's enough witnesses back in town," Max shouted, "including me."

"That's right," Laurie added. "The circuit judge'll do the deciding. Now — hands."

Minutes later the renegade was shackled with a loop of rope round a tree and through the cuffs. Unencumbered by his prisoner, Laurie knelt down to investigate the fate of his friend. He could see by the rent coat that the damage was in the arm. He opened the man's jacket and eased off the sleeve. Not as bad as he'd thought. The skin on the outer part of the arm was scored.

"Is nothing, *mein herr*," Max said. "I got a bodyful of scars and that's the measliest one yet."

"Think you can handle a gun?" Laurie asked after he'd tied a bandanna round the limb and helped the man slip the arm back into the sleeve. "It's a long ways back and this bozo is likely to try every trick in the book."

Max looked hard at the man who had failed to back him when it had come to the crunch. "Do not worry about me, *mein herr*," he said, with a Teutonic emphasis on the 'me'.

13

"MA, Ma, the posse's coming back!" Johnny shouted, busting through the door. He had been playing marbles in the street with his friends and had spotted approaching horsemen. Upstairs Jessica dropped the linen she had been neatly folding when she had heard her son's voice, and ran downstairs. She joined her son at the end of the path to watch the advancing riders. She counted their number. Six. Surely there had been more than that? As they neared she could tell her husband wasn't amongst them.

"Where's Laurie?" she yelled at Norman when he was in hailing distance.

"He's staying on the trail of the renegade, Mrs Bolan."

"What happened?"

"It got too bad for us up in the mountains."

"Why didn't he come back then?"

"They figured two of them could still make good headway."

She clasped her hands together. "They? Who's with him?"

"Max. So don't worry, Mrs Bolan."

"That's right, Jessy," Red added. "Laurie couldn't have a better pardner out there. He knows the mountains better'n the main street here."

She didn't speak but watched the four riders continue into town.

"He'll be all right, Ma," Johnny said, running off to resume his game of marbles with his playmates.

★ ★ ★

Heller halted when he saw the gap in the trees. Now overgrown it looked like it had been a path sometime. He turned off the trail and worked his way up the slope between inhospitable jack pine. The higher he went the more difficult it became and he found himself having to keep his head down to avoid the stinging whip of low-level branches. He dismounted and trailed his horse. After a long climb he fetched up against sheer rock.

He tied the hackamore rope to an overhanging branch and left his horse in order to explore the chalky face. After a short spell he came across a dented, holed bucket. Then the broken handle of what once was probably a pick. Eventually he found the cave entrance. Some yards down the slope in the undergrowth he could discern an overturned skip. This was the disused Columbia mine.

After exploring the interior, he stood at the mouth and looked down, but the winding valley was obscured by snow-covered trees. Well, if he needed a hide-out, this place would do.

★ ★ ★

It was the next day. In the kitchen, Jessica Bolan picked up a pot-holder and moved to the oven. She opened the range door and half-turned, grimacing from the heat that reached out for her as from a dragon's maw. She flapped away some heat with her apron, then took out a large baking tin. After putting the cake to one side she carried two plates from the Welsh dresser and laid them on the table. The cutlery laid out, she returned to the stove and stirred a simmering pot.

With some agitation she went to the window and noted it was getting dark. Little Johnny was out playing. If the little rascal didn't come in soon of his own accord she would have to go fetch him. The fading light gave her a further concern: Laurie wasn't back yet. She'd been sick in her stomach as soon as he'd ridden out with the posse. Her spirits had risen when she'd seen the returning posse, but, when she learned Laurie was one of two men staying on the killer's trail, she'd almost collapsed with worry. Last night had been the first time she'd been in a bed without her husband in all often years. Did the darkening sky mean she was to have a second night in a lonely bed?

Was he all right? The men had said for her not to fret. Laurie had the best of partners in his task. There wasn't a better backwoodsman than the German. Trying to gain some comfort from this notion, she'd spent the rest of the day in household chores but it wasn't sufficient to take her mind off things.

There was a knock at the door. She dropped the spoon and without wiping her hands raced to the front of the house. Her heart pounded. It wasn't Laurie because he would have walked straight in. Who could it be at this time? Through the lace curtain she could make out the outline of a man. Her heart sank. Oh God, had something happened to Laurie?

Was bad news being brought to her? She threw wide the door. "Yes?"

The man moved straight in, closed the door with his foot and rammed the muzzle of a sixgun into her throat. "Don't scream, lady, 'cos I'll kill yuh."

She recognized the claw hand. "You're . . . you're . . . "

"That's right, ma'am, Heller," the man said, giving her the word she was looking for. "The name's Heller. We've met before, kinda briefly." He prodded some with the gun. "Now, back away from the windows."

She complied.

"Where is he?"

"My husband? He's out. Due back any minute."

He laughed, then said, "Sit down," pushing the gun again. She withdrew into the sitting area and lowered herself on to a settee. "That's right, lady," he said. "Take it easy, and don't do anything stupid."

A sneer came to his lips as he continued. "I've already found out your old man's out of town. And why. Chasing some lawbreaker. That's a laugh. I only asked the question to see if he'd married a liar like he is. Seems he has."

He looked around the room, laden with expensive furniture. A multi-coloured Indian rug hung from the wall and there were heavy drapes at the windows.

"My, my, sure done all right for hisself ain't he?"

"What do you want?"

He ignored her question. There was a framed picture of a boy on the mantel. "Got a kid, too," he said, a hunk of cynicism in his tone.

"No," she faltered. "That's my nephew. What do you want?"

"I wanna talk with your husband."

"Like you did in Miles City?"

"That's right."

"You mean you want to kill him."

He ignored her statement and, keeping his gun levelled, sat down on the richly-patterned settee opposite her. "Don't suppose you know when he's coming back?"

She shook her head. No point in lying any more. He seemed to know the answers to his own questions.

A moment's quietness was disturbed by the noise of distant hoofbeats. The man rose, still keeping the gun aimed at her, and moved to the window. Some long ways off a rider was cantering down the street. "Just passing," he said quietly, as if to himself. Then, louder, "But that makes me think. You might get callers. Your old man being what he is, you might even get the law calling, a deputy or something. OK, if anything like that happens while I'm here, you act natural and don't say a thing. Any trouble and I'll put a bullet in you and your caller if I have to. I got a good chance of getting clear. My hoss ain't too far away." He laughed. "And there ain't no sheriff to come a-chasing!"

"I thought you were in jail," she said in a weak voice.

"Ain't no slammer good enough to hold me for long, lady." He stepped back and appraised the kitchen, then motioned with his sixgun. "Let's move back to the kitchen. Don't cotton to these windows out front. It ain't so open there. "Sides, something smells real good in back."

He followed her through to the rear of the house.

"What's this?" he queried, looking at the table. "Two plates? And one not quite so big as the other. Hey, that kid in the picture *is* yours. Tut, tut, you been lying again, Mrs Bolan."

He continued appraising the table. "And you're expecting the tyke any minute. Yeah, I remember, there was some young kids playing marbles down the block. He must have been one of them. A kid, eh? Well, well. This is getting cosier and cosier."

He peered into the pot on the stove. "Ain't had a good meal for days." He crossed to the far end of the kitchen. "I'd be obliged if you'd pour me a bowl of that stew, Mrs Bolan, and put it on the table."

She nodded and went to the stove. From the corner of her eyes she could sense Heller watching her every move, his good hand tracking her with his gun.

"I'll stay up here 'case you get any fool ideas about throwing anything hot at me."

When she'd served the meal he made her stand well clear while he wolfed it down, his gun within easy reach. "What's your name, lady?" he asked as he delved into a second helping.

She hesitated, reluctant to part with something as personal as her name, then said, "Jessica."

"Jessica," he repeated.

She was right, she thought. Her name was defiled coming from his ugly mouth.

"Purty name," he went on. "Suppose folks call you Jessy?"

"Some."

"Well, Jessy, what do you know about me?"

"That Laurie arrested you many years ago. As a result of that you went to jail for a long time and now it seems you have a grudge against him."

"Is that what he told you?" he laughed hoarsely. "I figured it'd be something like that. Well, I'm packing a grudge all right. But that's the only truth in what he's said."

"My husband is not a liar. He's a good man. The best thing that has happened to Judgement Creek in a long time. Ask anybody. And the best thing that has ever happened to me. A man like you wouldn't understand that."

"You'd be surprised what I understand, lady."

He looked her over. "He's sure got you round his little finger. Listen, lady. Just 'cos a man's good-looking and talks smart, don't make him a good man. And just 'cos a feller's got a pug-ugly face like mine and

141

a twisted-up hand, don't make him all bad."

"I don't know what you mean."

"You really don't, do you?" He nodded to the chair the other side of the table. "Sit down, lady. I figure this is gonna come as a surprise."

14

HESITANTLY Jessica positioned herself in the chair.

"Your husband's name ain't Laurie Bolan," Heller went on. "Don't know where he picked that monicker up from. His real name's Albert. Albert Heap. Everybody called him Prince, you know after Prince Albert, the limey queen's sidekick. Waal, Prince and me used to ride together. Texas way. I'm going back ten, fifteen years. We rode the owl-hoot trail. You know what that means, lady. We were outlaws. We've lived by knocking places over. Stores, stages. We did OK, too."

"Laurie? An outlaw? Huh! You're out of your mind."

"We're from Texas, ma'am."

"Of course I know Laurie's a Texan."

"You know what they say: it's just

as natural for a Texan to take up stage robbing and horse stealing as it is for a duck to take to water. And that's the truth, ma'am. We wus hardcase outlaws."

She made a scoffing noise. "You expect me to believe all this?"

"Makes no never-mind to me what you believe, Mrs Bolan. I'm just telling you like it was. Anyways, we'd decided on a bank. We'd cased it and it looked an easy number. Was too. It's surprising how cooperative folks can be when they got a couple of guns pointing at 'em. We just went in, took the money and left. Couple of lawmen chased us for a spell but we'd allus made sure we'd got good hosses under us. We lost 'em and eventually hit this burg on the Sante Fe railroad, seventy miles on. Tired ain't the word for what we felt. Well, we had the money so we booked in at this swank hotel. Said we wus cattlemen. There wus a passel of drovers in town so we didn't look outa place. We took a little drink and

144

I remember we exchanged words with a drummer. He had a couple of large cases and was about the same build as Prince, but I didn't think nothing of it at the time.

"Anyways, we were real bushed, so we headed back to the hotel room and bunked down. I don't have to tell you how edgy Prince can be at times. The fact of the matter is, despite being tired he couldn't sleep. Left me snoring, went down for a drink. In some saloon he heard the scuttlebutt that a big posse was in town. We thought we'd lost 'em but they'd dogged us all right, just like hunting hounds that you can't shake off Even managed to rope in some federal boys too on account of us crossing State lines. Jeez, there was a damn army of the critters. So what did my pardner do?" He paused. "You got any tobacco around, lady? I could sure do with a smoke."

"No. Laurie doesn't smoke."

He grunted. "No," he said. "Milksop all round. Couldn't handle his likker either. Now, where was I? Oh, yeah. Prince had learned there was a late-night train making a short stop. I reckon he did a deal with the drummer for his spare change of clothing and his merchandise. Back in our room Prince stashed the loot in the drummer's cases and put on the man's suit. The critter would have been careful about not making any noise but it didn't matter 'cos I would have slept through an earthquake. Must have cleaned hisself up a piece too, had a shave and stuff. Anyways, seems he caught the late train dressed up in the dandy suit with our loot in the drummer's cases. Nobody even noticed him.

"Not long after that the posse jumped me. I get a little crazy sometimes. Huh, I was by myself, surrounded, and in my long-johns, and I decided to show 'em I didn't like being took! There was a shoot-out right there in the hotel, and that's how I got this."

He waggled his claw hand. "Bullet straight through the palm. Mashed up the bones and tendons. Anyways, the law found the empty saddle-bags in the room and a few bills lying around. At the trial the bank identified the bills as belonging to the haul and that was that. Five years in the slammer."

"If that was true, Mr Heller, you would have told your captors about your accomplice. You might have gained some remission. You had nothing to lose by telling the authorities about your confederate in crime."

He laughed again. "'Course I told 'em. I told 'em again when I figured out how he'd made his get-away. But made no never-mind. He'd disappeared into thin air. Didn't leave no trail for the dust to settle on. Made a clean scoot. The upshot was I served my time and came out a man with a crook hand, no use to man or beast. I've bummed around ever since. Then I saw this piece in a newspaper. Written by some easterner. Fanciful garbage about the tamers of the wild west. Cot a picture of the Sheriff of Judgement Creek.

Someone called Laurence Bolan."

She remembered the writer coming to town. He had been just riding through and had stopped for refreshment in the saloon. Always on the look-out for escapades he could write about, he'd asked about the town's history. One of the old-timers had had too much to drink and, thinking of the incident in that very saloon which had led to Laurie becoming sheriff, had started bragging of how Judgement Creek had a fast-draw peace officer. The others had kept quiet about it and tried to shut him up when he started, because the story of the lynching had never got out of town. They managed to shut him up eventually and glossed over the lynching bit but the writer wrote down some garbage about Laurie exhibiting a fast draw when facing a desperado. He wouldn't leave town until he got a photograph of Laurie. She remembered how unsettled Laurie had been about the picture being taken.

"Yeah," Heller went on. "Laurence

Bolan. But it was Prince all right. Little older, little fatter. But him."

She shook her head. "You got things wrong."

"No, lady. Like you can't believe my tale, I couldn't believe what I saw in that newspaper at first. A no-good becoming a sheriff. Then it sank in. Prince was allus the clever one. Perfect cover. Change of name, using the loot to become a respectable businessman. Then to clinch it, getting elected sheriff. Damn clever. Who would suspect a goddamn lawman?"

"I still don't believe any of it. If what you say is true, and you had a confederate who made off with some loot, you'd be looking for your share of the money, not just to kill him."

He banged the side of his temple angrily. "I want *that* satisfying, lady. The gnawing in there. All these years. Money — zilch! Too late for that to mean much to me now."

"I think you're just a crazy man."

Her voice fell as she completed the sentence and saw how he glowered at her.

"Like I told you, lady, I don't give a rat's tail what you think."

"If you really thought Laurie was this criminal you'd expose him."

He laughed without humour. "No, there's only one way to handle this."

A little hope flashed in her eyes. "Listen. Instead of taking the law into your own hands, take your case to the authorities now."

He laughed again and looked around the room at the furnishing. "Given the situation, it'd be even more futile. I'm still a dirt bum and he's a big honcho with a badge and respectability. Talk sense, lady. Who'd believe me against him? I've told yuh, there's only one way to settle things now."

With that, he finished the rest of his meal in silence. Pushing the cleaned plate away he nodded at the coffee pot. "How about a coffee, ma'am? But no tricks.

"Didn't you ever wonder where his money came from?" he went on as she busied herself with the coffee pot. "A stranger rides into town, loaded with mazuma, and buys up half a street of stores?"

"He said he'd struck rich out in Virginia City."

"Virginia City, ha! The only time he was in Virginia City was when we were casing a mine there to knock over the payroll. And you believed him? Huh, the number of panners who make the big time, you could count on one hand."

"Yes, I believed him . . . because it's true."

He took his gun from the table and sheathed it. "True? How do you know, lady? Did you check? Have you spoken to anybody who knew him out in Virginia City?"

"I know *him*. He wouldn't lie."

"Huh. Tell you something else, lady. A feller doesn't learn how to handle a gun and fork a hoss like he does, panning for gold or scratching for silver ore."

"He'd served as a sheriff way back."

"Oh, yeah? Where? Did he say? Show documents? Or have any hard evidence to back up his story?"

"No." She hesitated and added, "But everybody knows."

"No, lady. Everybody *believes* him. There's a difference. That's 'cos he has a way with words. Allus did have."

Suddenly there was a scuffing of approaching feet outside. Small feet without much weight on them.

"That's the kid, ain't it?" Heller said.

She nodded, panic flaring across her face.

15

"JUST play along, lady, and nothing will happen," Heller said quickly and hard-toned. He patted his holstered gun as he spoke. "I've never harmed a kid before but there's a first time for everything. My life is already screwed up so I got nothing to lose. But remember, there's no need for the kid to be harmed, or even scared. It's in your hands."

As the man finished speaking the boy burst through the door. "Hi, Ma." He faltered when he saw the man at the table. "I thought Pa was home when I saw the horse, but then I saw it wasn't his."

"I'm your uncle, Son," Heller said in a change of voice. Your "Uncle Luke. Just coming visiting. Ain't that right, Jessy?"

She nodded. "Close the door, Johnny.

Wipe your feet and say hello to Uncle Luke."

"That's right," Heller said, with some satisfaction at her play-acting.

"I didn't know I'd got an uncle," the boy said. "You never told me about no uncle, Ma."

Heller chuckled. "Bright-looking kid. Handsome features like his pa. Well, I'm what they call the black sheep of the family. You know what that means, kid?"

"No, sir."

"Means kinfolk keep quiet about me. That's why you never heard of me."

"Why's that, sir?"

"You got naughty boys at school? Cheeky, sassing the teacher and stuff?"

"Yes, sir."

Heller winked. "Well, that's me. Naughty at school, and naughty ever since." He paused, putting his fingers into his vest pocket. "Uncles are supposed to be nice to their nephews. Here, kid." He spun a coin towards the boy.

The lad deftly caught it and held it up proudly for his mother to see. "Gee. Look, Ma. A silver dollar."

"Now get some food down yuh, kid. It's good stew. Your ma gave me some."

When Johnny was tucking heartily into his food, Jessica nodded to Heller to follow her into the front. "What are you going to do?" she whispered when they were out of earshot of the boy.

"Whatever you think of me, I ain't no back-shooter or a bushwhacker. I got a rifle and could have picked off your husband at Miles City. I hate him. Ten years is a whale of a time to build up a hatred but when I do it, it's gonna be face to face."

"Laurie's a sheriff and carries a gun but he's no pistol-artist. The wild days of Judgement Creek had long since gone when he was made sheriff. He's had little cause to use a gun. Most of his work as sheriff has been handling drunks. He wouldn't stand a chance against someone like you in a gun fight."

"You're forgetting this, Mrs Bolan," he said, shaking his claw. "This used to be my gun-hand. Good one, too. Sure, I've had time to teach my left hand things, like getting its fingers round a gun handle, but when your husband faces me it'll be a pretty equal face-up. Even mediocre, he stands as much chance as me of walking out of it. And that's a fact."

"If that's supposed to allay my fears, it hasn't succeeded."

"No, and I'll tell you one of the reasons why not. He's a bum and a coward."

"You got no call to say that."

"Hell, what do you know, woman? You yourself have told me he's never been tested while he's been carrying a badge in this hick burg. Doesn't take guts to handle a drunk. I told yuh, I rode with him for years. Plain across Texas and Kansas. Ain't nothing about his character I don't know. We did a lotta jobs together. He was always the talker. He could plan jobs. But when it came to the crunch, I was always up front. He's a double-dealer too. So don't let him do anything crazy over this business."

"What are you going to do?" she repeated.

"I had a mind to wait here for him. But with him wandering all over the territory it seems like it's going to be a long wait. Things could go wrong. He could turn up at the house with his deputy, anybody. And if it's gonna be a long wait you could panic when folks call and do something stupid. No, I'm gonna have to fix this so it's just me and him, like I said. With nobody to interfere or get in the way."

Their whispered conversation was interrupted by Johnny's voice from the kitchen. "Any more food, Ma?"

"Kid's got a healthy appetite," Heller observed. "That's good in a growing boy. You wanna make sure he keeps on growing, lady. It's in your hands."

Then he shouted in reply, "Your ma'll be along in a minute, kid."

He thought for a moment then continued in a lower voice. "I got an idea. I'm holing up in a deserted mine, The Columbia, some miles north east of the town. You know it?"

"I've heard of it."

"I'm gonna take Johnny back there."

"Oh, no," she spluttered, her voice rising.

"You OK, Ma?" the boy shouted.

"Yes, Johnny," she replied, managing to control her tone so as not to upset her son.

"Like I said," Heller went on, "I take Johnny."

"Please, take me instead. But not Johnny."

"Won't work that way. Now, listen up and don't get hysterical on me. I mean that. Believe me, blasting the two of yuh would be a darn good way of my getting back at Prince. Strikes me a fistful of heartache might be a better punishment for the critter than killing him. So don't persuade me that's the thing to do." He stared at her. "Now, have you calmed down?"

"Yes."

"Right. Like I said, I take the kid. You talk him into it, so there ain't no trouble. I might only be one-handed, but I could slug the pair of you and carry him out there across my saddle. So, convince him it's all right. I keep telling you, if there's no double-dealing the kid won't get hurt."

"I don't know what to say," she said weakly.

"You say yes." Then, "He got his own horse?"

She nodded. "A pony."

"Good, he can go on that. The idea is, we make it a fun thing for him. When the time comes I want you to put a pack of food together. Something to drink. And some blankets and stuff."

She leant weakly against the wall, looking at the ceiling. "Have you got to do this?"

"It's the only way, lady."

"I'll never forgive myself if I say yes and anything happens to him."

"It's better than any alternatives. We all gotta do unpleasant things in our lives sometime, Mrs Bolan. Me taking the boy is good for him in the long run."

He watched her whimpering for a few seconds and then said, "You mentioned money early on and I said I wasn't interested. But it's made me think. I could do with some. Gimme fifty dollars."

"You'll take that and go?" she asked expectantly.

"Don't be stupid, woman, just get it and put it in an envelope."

"In the study," she said.

He followed her into the next room where she opened the roll-top of a writing bureau. From a box she counted out fifty dollars and slipped them into an envelope.

"Now let's get back in the kitchen," he said as he pocketed it. "The kid's starving. And my coffee's going cold."

Back in the kitchen he looked on as the boy had a second helping. "Wanna go on an adventure, kid?" he asked after a while. "Just you and me?"

The kid's eyes were big and innocent. "Where to, Uncle?"

"Out to my place. We can take food and blankets for the trail. Have us an adventure. Something to tell your pals when you get back to school."

"Can I, Ma? Can I go with Uncle Luke?"

Jessica was having a problem holding back the emotion. "Yes. Of course."

The boy's pleading eyes noted something in her demeanour he didn't understand. "Something wrong, Ma?"

"I'm just worried about your father being away so long."

"Don't worry, Ma. He'll be back soon. Pa can handle himself. And he's got Big Max with him." The lad scooped up the last of the stew in the bowl. "When do we go, Uncle Luke?"

★ ★ ★

Jessica walked up and down the room clenching and unclenching her hands. Heller and Johnny had been gone an hour. She knew she'd done a bad thing. But what else could she do? Heller was a mean man. A desperate man. He might have killed the two of them there and then. And all those lies he'd told about Laurie. Heller was a no-good and a liar. He was on the run and liable to say anything. Why had she trusted a liar like that with her son? Because there was nothing else for her to do.

But Laurie wouldn't see it that way. Occasionally he 'blew his stack' as he called it and she knew he would do so when she told him she'd allowed Johnny to go with Heller. What were you thinking of, woman? she could hear him say. And she didn't know how she could answer him. Her action did seem stupid now. If anything happened to Johnny out there it would be her fault.

For the second time in her life she experienced panic. The first time had been on that boardwalk in Miles City. Then she had felt frightened and helpless. She felt those bad emotions now, but in addition she felt lonely. She sat in the drilling silence of the house. Wait, it wasn't too late. She could tell the deputy what had happened. She had to tell someone. The burden was getting too great for her shoulders.

She donned her shawl and set out for the law office.

"Evenin', Mrs Bolan," Norman said as she closed the door behind her. "What can I do for you?"

She looked at the young man sitting at Laurie's desk. She doubted if the smooth baby features had felt a razor yet. What would he know about handling a situation like this? Laurie was always complaining about his incompetence. Wasn't the young man's fault. He was just immature. There was only one man in town who would know what to do in circumstances like these. Max. But he was away with Laurie.

"Can I help you, ma'am?" Norman prompted, conscious of a delay in her response. "Hey, anything wrong?"

Of course, something was wrong, you young fool. Her husband had been away for two nights chasing a killer and the whipper-snapper asks her if anything is wrong! At that point she knew there was no way she could tell Norman what had happened. If she did, he was liable to do something impetuous. Now he had had the experience of forming a posse there was every chance he would pull one together again and ride out to Columbia and then who knows what Heller would do to Johnny.

"I just came to see if there was any news about Laurie."

"No, not yet, ma'am, I'm afraid."

She nodded, bade him goodnight and left. Norman was just a boy with a badge.

16

IT was the afternoon on the next day when the lawman and his partner rode into town with their prisoner. Norman came to the door at the sound of the horses.

"Wire the circuit judge," Laurie said as he dropped down from the saddle.

"Wire's still down, Laurie," Norman said.

"Hell," the sheriff grunted, stretching his limbs. "And the mail hack ain't due for three days."

He wasn't to know it, but lack of communication was only the beginning of his problems. As he marched Wilson through the law office door they were spied by the first citizens who scurried away to spread the news.

Minutes later Wilson was behind bars and the sheriff had warmed himself at the stove and got his aching backside on his desk. "Don't like having to wait for the mail hack. By the time the message arrives and the circuit judge has to fit this business into his schedule, then gets his ass out here . . . Hell, we could have that bastard on our hands for a week, mebbe two."

"We can handle that," Norman said with the optimism associated with lack of understanding.

Laurie shook his head. "Norman, a couple of weeks is a long time. With somebody like that varmint boxed up you don't know what can happen. He'll be as wily as a fox. We'll have to have at least two men on guard here night and day. And another thing, we don't know if he's got partners in the territory."

He rubbed his face. "Jeez, I'm tired." He eased himself off the desk and went to the window. "There's already a crowd building up outside. Where are they all coming from? Hell's teeth, we can't stop the news getting out now. If the jasper has got buddies within fifty miles they'll soon learn about this. Ain't no way we can stop 'em finding out."

"You can send a rider," Max said. "That'll cut the delay in the judge coming down to a matter of days."

Laurie nodded. "Yeah. There's gotta be somebody in town we can rely on who's a good rider."

"*Ja*," Max said. "There's a couple."

"I'll think it over," Laurie said. "In the meantime, Norman, look after the horses while I get home to see the missus and kid." He walked towards the door. "Help yourself to coffee, Max."

Before he got to it there was a knock at the door and it was opened without invitation. It was Red and Pete. They bustled in, closing the door on the rumble of voices behind them. "Hear you brung Wilson in," Pete said.

"Yeah," Laurie said. "He's in back."

The two visitors walked along the corridor and looked the prisoner over. "That's him all right," Pete said. "I'd know his plug-ugly face anywheres."

By the time the two returned to the front a commotion could be heard outside. "Can you hear 'em?" Red asked, nodding to the front door. "They wanna string him up now."

Laurie went to the window. "Huh, I might have knowed. Whenever there's trouble, Barney O'Hagan is plumb in the centre of it." The man he had named was standing at the head of a crowd of around ten, a noosed rope in his hand. Laurie opened the door and stepped out with Max to his rear. "What do you want, Barney?" he challenged.

"Wilson," O'Hagan said, wielding the rope as he stepped up on to the boardwalk. "You've done your piece, Sheriff. We appreciate that. But now it's our turn."

"The hell it is," Max snapped, stepping forward to stand alongside the sheriff.

"Max is right," Laurie went on.

168

"The handling of this is up to the circuit judge."

"It's murder, Sheriff," another man said. "That means it'll be a jury job. Don't matter which twelve men from Judgement Creek he picks, it'll be a unanimous verdict. We string him up now, that'll save everybody a passel of trouble."

"Hold your hosses, Barney," Max shouted above the growing hubbub. "I been in Judgement Creek as long as any of yuh, since it was a couple of shacks around a mud track. But we're a civilized community now. We elected Laurie to look after things like this. Things have gotta be done proper."

"Can't have no lynchings," Laurie added.

"Whose side you on, Bolan?" O'Hagan snarled. "The son-of-a-bitch killed our mayor!"

"And don't forget Manny!" someone else added.

Laurie looked at the big trapper for a moment, as if for direction, then back at the crowd. "Listen. The bozo's in custody and he'll get his deserts. But it's gonna be done the legal way. Now, if you don't disperse in one minute, I'll put you all in the slammer for breach of the peace."

Somebody laughed. "The jail ain't big enough, Sheriff."

That was true.

"Scat, all of you," Laurie shouted, jerking his head backwards as an indication to Max. The two men nipped quickly back through the doorway and Max slammed the bolts home once they were safely inside. The ensuing noise outside indicated the mob hadn't scatted. "They mean business, Laurie," he said, his back against the door.

"What's gotten into the folk?" Norman stammered.

"We seen it before, ain't we, Laurie?" Max said. "Half a dozen years back, when that varmint shot the sheriff. Crowd strung him up. Barney led that one too."

"Yeah," Laurie went on. "Listen to

'em. When I got back from Miles City, Norman couldn't get a posse together. Nobody was interested when it came to a man's job. So we eventually get one together, then most of 'em quit at the first sign of problems. Now the jasper's safely in the slammer without his weapons they wanna string him up. Like you say, Max, we seen it all before."

He flicked his hat on to the desk. "Norman, get over to my place and tell the missus I'm back. She'll be worried. Tell her I'll be over as soon as I can get free here. Don't tell her about this spot of trouble. She'll be fretting enough."

"Yes, sir." But as the deputy moved there was thumping on the door, hostile faces appearing at the two windows. He halted. "They're in a nasty mood out there, Sheriff. If I open that door they'll all be in and there won't be nothing we can do."

Max caught the nonplussed look that came to the sheriff's face. "We can't let 'em have Wilson," he said. "You know that, don't yuh, Laurie?"

"It's your duty to look after my welfare, Sheriff," the prisoner shouted from the back.

Laurie paused for a moment. He took out his gun and looked at the other two. "You guys with me?"

Both nodded, Max positively, the deputy less so.

"OK," the lawman said hesitantly. Then he raised his gun and fired an upward shot. The slug embedded itself in the door lintel, the explosion deafening in the enclosed space and certainly heard by those outside. Then he shouted through the crack in the door, "Listen up, you bunch out there. I'll shoot anybody who forces their way in!"

17

IT was a quarter-hour later. "They ain't going," Norman said, following another silent exchange with glowering faces through the window. The three men had taken Winchesters from the rack and thumbed in loads. Then they had bided their time over coffee.

"There's only one way outa this, Laurie," Max said, putting down his drained mug. "The townsfolk have got respect for you but you need backing. The way they're getting hotted up they won't take anything from me. To men like Barney O'Hagan I'm just a no-good Kraut. Norman's just a kid. You need backing by somebody they'll listen to. There's some sensible guys in town. One of us should get out to them. They might be able to talk the puff outa the hot-heads."

"Who you thinking of?" Laurie asked.

Max shrugged. "Roy the Boy, Deaney. The crowd might come to heel if they see you being backed up by regular guys."

"OK," the sheriff said. "Anything's better than just sitting useless on our asses." He looked at his deputy. "It'll be up to you, Norman. Max and I will cover the door while you get out. OK?"

"Yeah."

"You know what you have to do? Find out the lads. Deaney should be in the livery. Roy the Boy will probably be in his kitchen. They'll have heard we're back but they've got their jobs to do and they probably don't know the trouble we got here. Bring 'em over, get 'em to talk some sense into the critters outside."

"OK, Sheriff."

The two men raised their guns while Norman prepared for his exit. "Make it quick, so we can bolt up the door

174

again," the sheriff said, positioning himself near the jamb. "OK."

The young man tensed himself. Then Laurie pulled back the bolts and Norman slipped out. The lawman slammed home the bolts again and stood listening to the raised voices. After a spell it became quiet again.

"Now we just wait," he said.

★ ★ ★

Another quarter-hour had passed when raised voices were again heard outside. "It's Roy," Max said, glancing through the window. After a spell the volume fell and the clipped tones of Roy's voice could be heard. At least the mob were listening to him. Laurie eased open the door.

Roy, still with his apron round his waist, was standing on the edge of the boardwalk, placating hands extended towards the crowd like he was playing an invisible piano. "If we haven't got justice here," he was saying, "we haven't got anything. Back in territorial capital they think we're hicks. Uneducated backwoodsmen. Montana's moving towards Statehood. That's not too far away and when it comes we want a say in our own affairs. We aren't going to get that control if they think we're still unlettered savages who can't handle their own affairs in a disciplined way."

"You're talking like one of them," someone shouted from the crowd.

"Of course he is, you bozo," Deaney said, stepping on to the boardwalk alongside his pal. "And so do I. I've growed up here. I'm one of the boys, like most of you. We've had our rough times. And we've had our fun times. But there comes a time when things have to be done proper, and this is one of them." He thumbed backwards. "I wanna see that mad killer swing, just like you do. But we gotta back Laurie and Norman. I ain't a gunner, never have been, but anyone thinks different to me and wants to take the law into his own hands, put down his gun and face me with his fists."

There were angry mutterings among the crowd.

"Don't you see we're right?" Roy continued. "Times are changing. You hang Wilson, and Laurie will sure-fire lose his job when the authorities hear about it. Then the federal marshals will move in, might even impose martial law. Either way we lose control of our own town. Take your guns back home. Leave this to the man we elected as peace officer."

At that it went quiet, there was some shuffling then one by one the crowd dispersed.

"Thanks, boys," Laurie said to the two intercessors when the last of the gathering was making his way along the street. "I'll get you both a drink next time I'm in the saloon."

"No need, Sheriff," Roy said. "Only doing our civic duty. Just like you were doing when you put a couple of days into trailing that varmint. Now, while we're here, anything else we can do?"

"We need to get a message to the Judicial Department about having Wilson in custody. Just as far as the nearest working telegraph office. I'd be obliged if you could organize a rider."

"Sure. I'll get one of the boys to do it. You must be bushed. Now things are quieted you want somebody to stay over here a spell?"

"I'd be obliged if you could relieve me and Max. We're both stove-up and I wanna get to see the missus."

"No problems, Sheriff."

Minutes later Laurie was taking off his gloves as he trudged up the path to his house. With a sigh of utter tiredness he pushed open the door and dropped his hat and gloves on a chair.

"Oh, Laurie," Jessica exclaimed, grabbing hold of him. "I heard you'd come back, then wondered why you didn't come home. I came to the office but there was an angry crowd outside. I couldn't get through."

"Yeah. A bout of mob fever. Don't worry, it's sorted now." He held her at arm's length. "Hey, what's the matter? You look terrible. You been crying."

She fell against him. "It's Johnny. That man from Miles City, Heller. He came and took Johnny."

His face changed. "Johnny? Heller? I thought he was in jail?"

"He said he broke out."

"How come we didn't know?"

"The city marshal might have tried to warn us but the telegraph lines are still down."

"Jeez, I was forgetting. Anyways, what do you mean, he took Johnny?"

"Said it would make you come for him."

"Where?"

"What you gonna do, Laurie?"

"What you mean, what am I going to do?" He said irritatedly. "For Crissakes, tell me, woman, where?"

"First, you've got to tell me what you're gonna do."

"Listen, woman, half the fellers in town are riled up for blood. We've just managed to quiet 'em down for a spell.

I'll tell 'em about Heller making off with my kid. There'll be no problem of volunteers for a posse. We'll ride out and get him. Then they can have their blood and we'll be finished with the no-good Heller once and for all."

"No, it can't be like that. Heller says just you alone. He's made it plain, he sees anybody riding with you and he'll kill Johnny."

"I can keep the posse behind me out of sight."

"No, Laurie. We can't risk that. For Johnny's sake. Just you. That's my condition."

"You can't bargain with me. We're talking about our son here. Hell, what's got into you, woman? Now where?"

"Only if you promise you'll go out alone."

Laurie dropped on the settee, his head in his hands. His wife sat beside him. "He said some things," she went on. "About you."

Laurie raised his tired head. "What you mean, things?"

"About you and him being bad men, a long time ago."

He laughed cynically. "He's just shooting off his lip. Trying to set you against me. Cause trouble. Confuse things."

"I know."

"Now where did he take Johnny?"

"The old mine. The Columbia."

Laurie sat quiet, now and again moving agitatedly, rubbing his leg, wiping his face.

Jessica's agitation showed itself in incessant wringing of her hands. "I know you're tired, Laurie," she said after a spell, "but you've got to get out there. Now."

Laurie rose, breathing heavily, and walked to the door without a word.

"What you gonna do?" she asked, following him. "You still haven't told me. You are going by yourself, aren't you? I know you're tired but you've got to go alone. We've got to put Johnny first." Her voice was cracking. "Please, say you won't take anyone with you."

His face expressionless, he put on his hat. "Don't worry, Jessica. I'll go alone. With that shot-up gun-hand of his, I should be able to handle him."

She pondered on his words, then she grabbed his arm. "Shot-up hand?" There was an accusing look in her eye. "How did you know it was shot-up? You told me you thought he must have injured it somehow in prison."

"I just guessed."

She watched as he picked up his gloves. She stayed him as he began to put them on. "You came to Judgement Creek with a lot of money. Where did you get enough to buy up businesses?"

"That's a damn odd question. Struck it rich in Virginia City like I told yuh. You know that."

"I only know it because you told me."

"Jessy, I ain't the one on trial here, for Crissakes."

She took one of his ungloved hands and examined the palms, the fingertips. The soft hands that she had loved to feel running over her body. "You don't get hands like this panning for gold or scratching for ore in the ground."

"What is this?" he said, nonplussed. "And where d'you get words like that? Don't sound like you talking at all."

No, she thought, and you don't sound like my husband. Or look like the Laurie she had known. He was looking worn. She knew one thing: the last few days had aged him.

He finally pulled on his gloves but she prevented him opening the door. "He *was* lying, wasn't he, Laurie? Tell me he was lying. About the two of you."

"Hell, woman. 'Course he was," he said, wrenching the door from her grasp. "You can allus tell when he's lying. His lips move." He heavy-footed on to the porch. "Who you gonna believe, me or him?"

"He said that, too," she said as her husband lumbered down the path.

18

HE staggered down the street towards the law office. A couple of guys bade him goodnight as they passed but he didn't hear them. He paused in the fading light at the hitch-rail. What the hell was he to do? Heller was no fool. For him to be offering a straight face-to-face shoot-out meant he would have done a lot of practising with that left hand of his. Probably snake-quick on the draw with it now; and a dead shot. In the light coming from the law once window he looked at his own hands. They were quivering. And his guts were screwed up tighter than a cork in a whiskey bottle. Whiskey, whiskey.

Yeah, whiskey. He could do with a drink. He sure needed something to settle himself while he thought things out. He'd got a bottle in the law office but he couldn't face the company of the greenhorn in there. Damn incompetent milksop with his mouthful of platitudes. He changed course and headed for the Market Saloon.

He was greeted with "Hey, Sheriff," as he entered. It was Barney O'Hagan. "Sorry about that business outside your office today. Just got carried away."

Similar apologies came from other parts of the room. But the return of sanity to the town's hot-heads was lost on the lawman.

"Hey, you OK, Sheriff?" O'Hagan went on. "You don't look too good. Figure you're overworking yourself. You gotta relax more."

Laurie stumbled towards the bar without speaking.

"Here, have a drink," O'Hagan suggested, indicating the opened bottle of rye in front of him. "On me."

"Won't say no," Laurie said, leaning on the bar. "Obliged."

O'Hagan waved to the new barman

who passed across a clean shot glass. "Of course, the Englishman was right," O'Hagan said, as he poured a full measure. "We gotta do things right and proper. What we did last time was wrong."

Noting that the lawman downed the drink in one, he pushed the bottle towards him. "Help yourself," he added. "You must be in need of that, being out in rough country for two days and all. The chinook is warming up the days but it must get cold out there at night."

"Sure does," Laurie said, half listening.

Someone the other side of the room mentioned a game of cards.

"Yeah, that's an idea," O'Hagan said. "Help you take your mind off things, Sheriff."

"Not for me," Laurie said, shaking his head. "I'm real stove-up like you said."

"Understood, pal," O'Hagan said, rising to join the others. "You don't mind if I do?"

"No."

"Keep the bottle," the other said, heading across the room. "I'll get another. Least I can do after the trouble we caused you today when you got back."

"Obliged," Laurie said, and took the bottle to a vacant table, relieved to be alone at last.

"No hard feelings?" O'Hagan shouted as he joined his pals.

Laurie wished the goddamn guy would shut up. "No hard feelings," he echoed. He stared unseeing into the replenished glass, oblivious to the noise coming from the start of the game. What the hell was he to do? His brain groped for an answer. He couldn't face Heller. No matter what he'd said to Jessy. If he told these guys here, they would come with him. They could flush Heller out together. Despite the owl-hoot's warning to Jessy about shooting Johnny, he knew Heller enough to know that he was bluffing. He wouldn't shoot a kid. He'd ridden with him long enough to know that. Heller was an evil-looking bozo but he'd got a soft spot for things like kids, stuff like that.

No, Heller hurting Johnny wasn't the problem. The problem was, doing the job with a posse, Johnny could get hit accidentally in the cross-fire. Even get killed. In a tight corner Heller had the guts to take on any number, like he'd done in that hotel room.

No, if Johnny got injured . . . Laurie would find that hard to live with. And he'd have to answer to Jessy for taking a posse out there when she'd made him promise not to. She'd never forgive him. His days in Judgement Creek would be over. His comfortable days. His happy days.

His mind combed the ins and outs of the situation. This was an unwanted drama. He glanced at the clock, aware of the tension throughout the whole of his body.

Jeez, why had Heller come back? He'd got it so well made here. Happy marriage and a kid. Businesses which ran themselves. He'd done a good stint as sheriff and was in line for mayor. God, his old partner had got a long memory. He thought those days were long gone. Of course, way back, when he was starting up a new life, he had kept a watchful eye over his shoulder for anything which might have come creeping up on him from his past. But so much time had passed Laurie had become complacent and had utterly forgotten about Heller. He threw back another drink. What was he to do? If he wasn't so danged tired, maybe he could think straight.

The ticking of the clock got louder, tormenting him, shouting at him that time was passing fast. He rubbed his forehead slowly, firmly, continually, as though trying to rub his thoughts away. Before long he was looking at an empty bottle. And then, in the thick distorted glass, he saw the answer.

19

BACK in the law office Norman was sitting in Laurie's chair, feet on the desk. He swung his legs down and jumped up as his boss came through the door.

"Listen," Laurie said, "you must be tired." He did his best to cover up the effects of drink on his speech. "You been on duty for three days now. Get yourself home to bed. I'll take over here."

"You're more tired than me, Laurie. You been riding for two days."

"Yeah, I know. But I'm all wound up; nerves as tight as a drum. Can't sleep. May as well put my time to good use. Now, you get yourself home. Bunk down, get some shut-eye."

"You sure, boss?"

"I'm sure," Laurie said, taking off his hat and moving round to the back of his desk to drop into the now vacated chair.

"OK," Norman said, getting a grip of his own hat. "You're the boss. I've just put a couple of logs in the stove. Should see you through. See yuh in the morning."

The sheriff waved a hand as his deputy disappeared through the door. He sat listening to the clump of boots on the boardwalk. When it was quiet outside he crossed to the door and threw the bolts. On his way back to his desk he collected a bottle and glass from a cupboard. Alter he had poured himself a drink he looked at the clock. Too early yet. There was time to kill. Now his mind was eased with a plan it was only another couple of drinks before he was asleep.

His bladder prompted him into wakefulness as he knew it would. His eyes opened. The clock said half two. A couple of hours before dawn. Perfect. He washed his mouth with another couple of whiskey shots then moved down the corridor to the privy. He looked in the cell as he passed. Wilson was lying on his bunk, swathed in blankets, eyes closed. The lawman emptied his bladder and returned to the passageway.

He leant on the cold wall opposite the cell. "You asleep?"

Wilson's eyes fluttered open. "Not now." He worked his head around, taking in the scene with a shuddery, blinking just-woken-up look. "Hell, it's still dark. What time is it?"

"Half two."

"Damn cold too. That stove burnt out?"

Laurie ignored the question. "You been lucky so far, Wilson."

"Lucky? Shivering behind bars in a hick dump like this?"

"Yeah, lucky there was only two of us caught up with you. If we'd had the rest of the posse with us, you'd have been shot out of hand. You heard the rabble out there today. The townsfolk are baying for your blood."

"I heard 'em."

"We had a similar situation here a few years back. Some hardcase passing through shot and killed the sheriff. An important man in the town. Like the mayor you put a bullet in. Mob got real nasty, bust in here and dragged the prisoner out. You seen that tree just as you ride in. Outside Deaney's Livery Stable. Hung him from that."

Wilson turned his back to the speaker and pulled up the blanket.

"That bunch today," Laurie went on. "We managed to quiet 'em down but they could erupt again any time. Wouldn't be surprised if we had some more trouble in the morning. Don't know how long I can keep 'em off."

The prisoner nestled his head further into the blanket womb. "It's your duty to look after me while I'm in your custody, Sheriff."

"Yeah, I know. I'll do my best to stop 'em stringing you up but we're gonna be in this situation for a long time. There's only these bars and that wooden door between you and them. The telegraph wires are down and we can't notify the Judicial Department as quick as we'd like. We could be stuck like this for a week or more."

"So?"

"If we can manage to keep 'em off you, you know what's gonna happen then. When the circuit judge does come, the trial's gonna be a formality. Whatever happens you're gonna get strung up anyhow."

"You ain't telling me nothing I don't know."

"Got a proposition."

Wilson turned and raised his head on his elbow. "You got a proposition? For me?"

"Yeah. The guys tell me you look like you're good with a gun. And up in the mountains you were pretty snappy when we took you into custody."

"I can look after myself."

"Waal, it's this way. There's another hardcase I want getting shed of. Hard to imagine, but more trouble to me than you are. Now, if you could eliminate him for me, and by eliminate I mean dead meat, make no bones about that, you could have your freedom.

"You want *me* to kill somebody for me to go free? Sounds a crazy notion to me.

"The only straw you got."

"How would you work a deal like that?"

"Simple. I'd give you your guns, open the door and tell you where the critter is. Your horse and rig are out back. I'd tag along after a spell to check you had followed your end of the deal. Once I was sure you'd fixed the bozo's wagon for good and all, I'd see to it that you'd have a clear trail."

"How d'you swing that?"

"I'm the sheriff, ain't I? For the look of it I'd have to get a posse together. Ride out, like before, but this time I'd take 'em the wrong way."

"I don't get this. You, a lawman, want me to gun a man down?"

"That's the size of it."

"Why?"

"I got my reasons. Don't care how you do it."

Wilson pondered on it. "This smells. It ain't a set-up so you can kill me escaping? A way of getting me outa your hair? I've heard of that kind of trick."

"Talk sense. If I wanted you outa my hair that easy, I'd have let the lynchers in. Or even more easy, shot you up in the mountains."

Wilson thought on it some more. "Might be interested."

"But I give you warning. If you just vamoosed, the chase would be on again. A no-nonsense lynching party this time. But it wouldn't get as far as a rope if I was there when they got to you. I'd make sure you got gunned down before you had time to shoot your mouth off about our deal. There's already a dodger on you. If somehow you got away from the posse the townsfolk can give a good description of you. It would be circulated and no place in the territory would be safe for your hide. No matter how long you holed up."

The prisoner swung his feet off the bunk and sat up, keeping the blanket over his shoulders. "Listen. We both got a brain in our heads. You must know I could blast you once you've let me out and put a gun in my hand."

"That's a chance I'll have to take. We're gonna have to trust each other on this. But gunning down a mayor and a sheriff, you'd have a posse on your tail for the rest of your natural."

Wilson stared at him. "You don't look nuts." Then, "If there's a double-cross when I've planted this feller, I'd kill you. I ain't joshing when I say I can use my irons. You know it."

Laurie breathed deep. "No double-cross."

"OK, Sheriff. It's a deal." He cast a hard glance around his cramped cell. "Ain't got nothing to lose."

Laurie went back to the front and returned with his keys. By the time he got back the prisoner had shucked his blankets and was standing shivering, waiting for him. The sheriff opened the barred door and Wilson accompanied him to the front office. For a moment they both warmed their hands at the stove.

"There's your weaponry," Laurie said, pointing to the gun rig hanging from a hook. "Your hat and mackinaw."

He took another drink and rested his backside on the desk while he watched the ex-prisoner sling the belt around his hips and buckle it. "Once you're through that back door you're gonna have to take your chances getting outa town," the lawman said. "You could be seen. But it's early morning and still dark so you should get clear OK. I'll have to let you ride off alone a spell. I can't afford to be seen with you."

Wilson deftly pulled the guns to remind himself of the feel and for a second he looked menacing. He checked the loads and as he donned his outer clothes, Laurie explained how to get to the Columbia.

20

LAURIE opened his eyes. He was sitting at his desk, head resting on his arms. Hell, he wasn't used to booze and couldn't take it. With the amount he'd washed down his throat he'd dropped off to sleep again. The coldness told him there wasn't much left of the fire. He pulled his brain together and looked at the clock. Over an hour since Wilson had gone. He hadn't intended to wait this long. He heaved himself out of the chair. He wrapped himself up in his big overcoat, checked his side guns, then took a Winchester out of the rack.

A couple of minutes later he was heading out of town. At least there was no light yet and nobody about. In vain he scoured the trail as he rode. With the darkness and no recent fall of snow, he couldn't detect any evidence of Wilson's having passed. Within half an hour came signs of the first dawn, high clouds catching the light from the still hidden sun creeping up behind the eastern ranges. Then, shortly and suddenly, the sun itself sent spears of light from the mountain tops.

The break in the trees marking the trail to the Columbia was clear enough. Before turning up it he dismounted and made a more rigorous study of the ground. Still no sign of a rider. Was it Wilson's plan to circle round and come on the Columbia from an angle? Or had the jasper vamoosed? The ground was still hard and there was no way of telling. He climbed back into the saddle and headed up the disused trail to the mine, with the sun now inching its way upward through the trees.

He was puzzled. Wilson had had plenty of time to carry out his task. In the stillness of the morning Laurie would have heard any gunfire way down the trail. The sound would have racketed down the valley. Yet he had heard nothing.

Well before the clearing that marked the mine's entrance he dismounted again and tethered his horse. Slowly he advanced on the site. He stayed under cover and surveyed the scene. Long abandoned detritus: a crumbling wagon, rotting props scattered around. But no sign of horses. No sign of anybody. Not to mention Heller's splayed-out lead-heavy body, the sight which he was really paining to see.

He squinted and studied the hole in the distant rock. Still no sign of Wilson either. Indeed, no indication of anyone having been there. Had Heller been playing straight? Keeping to the trees he circled the open space, right round until he got to the rock face. He took out his gun. He pulled the hammer full back and the chamber revolved, lining up the first loaded chamber. He held the gun in readiness and worked his way slowly along the wall, regularly glancing at the surrounding trees.

At the mine entrance he paused, then carefully looked into the maw. Nothing. Gingerly, careful to avoid the crunching of gravel, he advanced into the darkness. He was conscious of the sweat under his arms, in the small of his back, between his gloved fingers. Sweat that seemed to turn to ice in the cold air. Now and again he would pause, listening for any sound coming from the depths that would indicate occupation. Breathing, movement, anything.

Thirty feet in, the vestiges of light from the entrance disappeared, leaving complete blackness ahead. Nothing but a mustiness coming up to his nostrils from the depths. No point in going any further. Nobody had been here for some time. Not Heller, or Johnny. Nobody.

In the darkness he mulled over the situation. There would be no reason for Heller to entice him to the mine and yet not be there himself. Even if it was to shoot him on his approach.

He dismissed that notion. His old owl-hoot partner could have picked him off on the trail from Miles City. No, he wanted a straight face-to-face match. That's what he'd told Jessy. And that's the kind of guy he was anyway. Lived by a code of sorts, even though he was a crook. Yes, Heller had to be about somewheres ready to play this out straight.

Then a possibility crossed his mind. How stupid of him to forget. Several times he'd brought Johnny up here on hunting trips. He ought to have remembered. There were two entrances! The other was a couple of hundred yards to the east. Come to think of it, it was bigger than this one but he'd forgotten about it because it had been disused for longer and had become overgrown, without a flattened clearing before it like this one, not immediately apparent. And which one a traveller came on first depended on what direction he made the approach. More, the two entrances weren't in sight of each other. He mentally kicked himself, then began to feel his way back towards the entrance.

* * *

Wilson was irritated. The lawman back in Judgement Creek had said the mine was easy to find once you'd left the trail. But coming up from the valley he had lost his way in the trees. Several times while he had been stumbling through the bracken he had thought of turning around, heading back and taking his chances by lighting a shuck outa here. This was a damn fool caper anyhows. The lawman back in that hick town was crazy.

But, each time the thought had hit him, he'd told himself to stay with it. Although the lawman was crazy he probably meant what he'd said about letting him make a getaway if he shot this feller down. He had to play it; it was his best chance.

It had taken him a long time, first

upward towards the heights commanding the valley, then cutting across the mountainside, this way and that, before he had found it. A large clearing, the signs of some long-gone industrial activity. When he spied the mine entrance itself he smiled to himself and levered his Winchester.

★ ★ ★

Heller was tired and cold. All night he'd stayed some yards back inside the tunnel with only a blanket around him, waiting, listening. Occasionally he'd dropped into a half-sleep, but it had only been for minutes at a time. Prince didn't know it but his chances were stacking up higher and higher. In the final gundown he was gonna be facing a man with a useless right, a not-too-good left, fatigued, and his whole body aching and stiff with cold.

He smiled cynically to himself. Even if Prince was acquainted with the facts of his condition, he'd still be a scared jack-rabbit. No guts unless somebody was backing him up. Nevertheless, Heller was increasingly reconciling himself to the big chance that this was probably his last day. But it didn't matter. This was the way he wanted it. If he managed to put just one slug into the yellow sidewinder before he went, it would be worth it.

Dawn came, nothing. Then he heard the noise. The mine entrance was catching the sound coming up the slope and magnifying it along its rocky tunnel. Down below, someone stumbling about through the undergrowth, crunching frozen stems underfoot. Prince!

He stood up and shucked the blanket, working his stiff limbs. He tried to shake some life into his left hand, then took out his gun. He braced himself and edged forwards, his hearing concentrated. By what he could hear he reckoned there was only one man and a horse. So, Prince wasn't bringing a posse. That was good. It was going to be the way he wanted it. One to one, face to face.

He'd meant what he'd said to the woman. Although he'd exercised his left hand over the years, it was a poor second to his skilled, fast right, now useless bone and cartilage.

But by the time he got to the entrance the sound was becoming fainter. Why would Prince be going past the entrance? Was the varmint intending to jump him? He wouldn't put it past him. He was a smooth bastard, and as nasty as a barrelful of rattlers.

Fully alert, he inched out of the mine. Nobody in view. The noise told him his visitor was still in the vicinity but he was moving westward across the grade. Making sure he could always pinpoint the noise, Heller emerged completely and worked his way along the rock face.

Eventually through the canopy of whitened branches he could make out another clearing. He couldn't make it out too clearly but there was some dark indentation in the rock. What did that mean? Were there two mines?

Then he saw the man who had been creeping through the forest. He'd tethered his horse and seemed to be waiting at the rim that dropped to the clearing. Whoever this was, it wasn't Prince. He could see enough to know that. It was some small feller. What the hell was going on?

Meanwhile, oblivious that he himself was being watched, Wilson waited behind the cover of a tree. He didn't have to wait long. From behind the tree trunk he could make out a figure appearing at the entrance to the mine. The man was turned so that Wilson couldn't see his right, couldn't see if he had a crook hand. But this must be the varmint the sheriff was after. OK, lawman, he said to himself as he raised the barrel, this is my end of the bargain. I hope you keep to yours. And he pulled the trigger.

The bullet shattered Laurie's ribcage

and he fell against the wall, loosing off one shot as he fell. Too late, Wilson saw the man was holding a gun quite capably in his right hand. The sheriff had described his hit as having some deformity in the right.

In the same second, Heller recognized the falling man as Prince. "You bastard!" he yelled at the bushwhacker and sprang from cover. "He was mine!"

Wilson turned. He swung his gun when he saw the figure with the claw hand coming out of the trees way above him but he was too late. Heller fired one shot which put a starred hole in Wilson's forehead. The man cannoned backwards, and slithered down the grade.

Heller heavy-footed down to the clearing and, gun levelled, advanced on the prone figure of the short man. Whoever he had been, he didn't have to bother about the runt any more, his shot had been a killing one. He loped over to the mine entrance where Laurie was groaning.

He dropped to one knee. He could see by the mess that had been the man's chest that his one-time partner wasn't going to make it. "Who the hell was that?" he asked, standing over the lawman.

"Just me being stupid, Luke," Laurie managed to say, weakly. "Where's Johnny?"

"He's OK, Prince. Staying with a friend of mine. I wasn't going to have him around where there was going to be gun-play. The kid was nothing to do with the trouble between you and me."

Laurie's eyes closed and he smiled faintly. "I ought to have known you wouldn't have put him at risk. Huh, Prince; ain't heard that name for a long, long time." Then he tried to say, "See the boy gets back safe to his ma." But he only got half-way through the sentence.

Heller stood up. "So long, Prince." In the cold air he pondered whether it had been worth it in the end. It hadn't fell the way he had intended, but does anything in life? He left the bodies where they lay and crossed the mountainside to relocate his horse. Leading the animal down the steep slope, he mounted up as it levelled out towards the trail.

First, he would make for the cabin, finish his business there. In his pocket he had an envelope containing fifty dollars. He would write Whitehead's name on it and post it care of the marshal, Miles City. That would be a surprise for the old-timer, not to mention the lawman. Stolen money returned? What was the world coming to? But a guy didn't have to be a shmuck all his life.

Then what? He hadn't made any plans beyond today. He'd had enough of this cold weather, that was sure. He'd head south, yes, least it was warm thataways. California, that was an idea. Maybe somebody could use a one-armed orange-picker. Hell, what a life.

21

IT was midmorning when Norman arrived at the Columbia with a posse. Turning up earlier for work he had found the law once empty. Both Laurie and the prisoner had gone. It was a real puzzle because there had been no sign of a break-out but the deputy had assumed Wilson had managed to pull some trick on the lawman. Hadn't Laurie himself said that, as a hardened criminal, Wilson would be as wily as a fox?

He made straight for the Bolan house but Laurie hadn't been home and he couldn't get any sense out of Jessy. She was in a hell of a state, so on the way back to the law office the deputy asked a neighbour to pay her a visit.

At the time Norman couldn't understand why Laurie hadn't given the alarm and raised a posse. But his horse had gone so he figured his boss must have set out in immediate pursuit, not wanting to lose time. Crazy, but everybody knew Laurie could be a mite pig-headed at times.

And another strange thing. He hadn't left a message about what had happened or in which direction he had gone. Had Wilson pulled some stunt and taken Laurie hostage?

Norman called the boys together and they talked it over. The best thing would be to send out search parties. It was just as they were organizing that when Roy the Boy came to the law office. A settler coming into town early to buy stores was having a bite to eat at his place and remarked that he'd heard shots. Out on the trail, the man had reported; seemed they came from the direction of the old Columbia mine.

Figuring it was something to do with the Wilson break-out, Norman pulled a posse together and headed out.

Well, when they got there they found two frozen bodies. Laurie's and

Wilson's. It was plain the prisoner had broken out somehow and Laurie had trailed him. The lawman had caught up with the varmint, there'd been a shoot-out and both had blasted each other.

That seemed to be that but back in town, there were one or two who had reservations. Max particularly. Yeah, on the surface the sheriff had been a straight-up guy, but . . . well, they kept their reservations to themselves.

* * *

Jessica hadn't slept all night. The whole thing was made worse because she couldn't tell anybody anything. Then she'd heard of the new trouble, of Wilson breaking out of jail during the night and Laurie going after him alone.

But her concerns were temporarily alleviated when Johnny unexpectedly turned up on his pony. The boy was tired and disappointed. His Uncle Luke hadn't taken him on an adventure at all, he complained. Just ridden him out of town and left him with a friend. Aunty Kathy, she was called. Nice lady living in a cabin, but it was no adventure. When he had woken up that morning Uncle Luke came back from somewhere, the boy didn't know where. The man had simply asked if the boy was big enough to get back to town alone. And that was it. No adventure at all.

The young lad didn't understand any of it, especially when his ma insisted he told no one of the incident. However, the relieved mother's joy was cut short when Norman came knocking at the door later that morning with real bad news.

Later that day there was a meeting of the town council and they fixed a handsome figure by way of some compensation to the sheriff's widow. It was the best they could do for an officer killed in the line of duty. In his last hour her man had shown himself to be a hero, shooting it out with a hardened criminal. The man would become a town legend.

That evening Jessica sat by the fire with some female neighbours who were staying overnight to comfort her. She had cried when learning of her husband's death. And she would cry for some time to come, but she was already accepting her loss. In some strange way, the events of the last few days had prepared her for it.

The ladies around the fire talked about the harshness of life and how time heals wounds. Stuff like that.

But she wasn't listening. She was thinking of how much she would tell Johnny.

As she looked into the flames, dancing their strange patterns in the fireplace, she knew she would not tell the boy the truth as she was beginning to understand it. It was a good and rare thing for a boy to think of his father as a hero.

Epilogue

ALL that was a long, long time ago. The seasons still come and go in the same way. I suppose the chinook still brings the warmth, heralding the spring. But Montana isn't the wild land of outlaws and shoot-outs any more. The territory became a State in 1889 and, although the mountains, forest and rivers are still there, big business, logging industries, factories are today's landmarks.

Ma married again. Roy the Boy, you remember him, the English feller. He was a good step-father to me and they had a happy life together. He helped with the stores that Ma had been left and she enjoyed getting involved with the eats-house business. Really made it fancy, giving it the woman's touch, insisting customers took off their hats and wore napkins.

I grew up, left Judgement Creek, had a family of my own. In fact, my missus tells me she thinks we're going to be grandparents pretty soon.

Yes, life's been good.

I enjoy my job and have a few years left before I retire. I'm a newspaper man, out in Helena, the big city.

And that's how come the other day I read a newspaper report of the death of an old man, a derelict in a charity hospital someplace out in California. I wouldn't have given it much mind but there were tales that he had been an outlaw and he was clearly quite old, claimed to be ninety. So it crossed my mind maybe we could use the event as a starting point to write a piece for the paper. You know the kind of thing, looking back at the old days.

I've got an especial interest in that type of story as my own pa was a law officer way back, said to be a legend in his time.

Anyway, what got me in the report about this fellow in the hospital were his dying words, something he said he'd never revealed before. A story of how he'd been a jailbird once, a long time ago when the West was really wild. And of how, when he came out, he spent ten years seeking out a double-crosser. And how he finally tracked down the man but in the final confrontation, his intended victim ironically was killed by some other jailbird.

The dying man didn't give any names but the report mentions he had a claw hand . . .

Other titles in the Linford Western Library:

TOP HAND
Wade Everett

The Broken T was big. But no ranch is big enough to let a man hide from himself.

GUN WOLVES OF LOBO BASIN
Lee Floren

The Feud was a blood debt. When Smoke Talbot found the outlaws who gunned down his folks he aimed to nail their hide to the barn door.

SHOTGUN SHARKEY
Marshall Grover

The westbound coach carrying the indomitable Larry and Stretch headed for a shooting showdown.

FIGHTING RAMROD
Charles N. Heckelmann

Most men would have cut their losses, but Frazer counted the bullets in his guns and said he'd soak the range in blood before he'd give up another inch of what was his.

LONE GUN
Eric Allen

Smoke Blackbird had been away too long. The Lequires had seized the Blackbird farm, forcing the Indians and settlers off, and no one seemed willing to fight! He had to fight alone.

THE THIRD RIDER
Barry Cord

Mel Rawlins wasn't going to let anything stand in his way. His father was murdered, his two brothers gone. Now Mel rode for vengeance.

ARIZONA DRIFTERS
W. C. Tuttle

When drifting Dutton and Lonnie Steelman decide to become partners they find that they have a common enemy in the formidable Thurston brothers.

TOMBSTONE
Matt Braun

Wells Fargo paid Luke Starbuck to outgun the silver-thieving stagecoach gang at Tombstone. Before long Luke can see the only thing bearing fruit in this eldorado will be the gallows tree.

HIGH BORDER RIDERS
Lee Floren

Buckshot McKee and Tortilla Joe cut the trail of a border tough who was running Mexican beef into Texas. They stopped the smuggler in his tracks.

BRETT RANDALL, GAMBLER
E. B. Mann

Larry Day had the choice of running away from the law or of assuming a dead man's place. No matter what he decided he was bound to end up dead.

THE GUNSHARP
William R. Cox

The Eggerleys weren't very smart. They trained their sights on Will Carney and Arizona's biggest blood bath began.

THE DEPUTY OF SAN RIANO
Lawrence A. Keating and
Al. P. Nelson

When a man fell dead from his horse, Ed Grant was spotted riding away from the scene. The deputy sheriff rode out after him and came up against everything from gunfire to dynamite.

FARGO: MASSACRE RIVER
John Benteen

The ambushers up ahead had now blocked the road. Fargo's convoy was a jumble, a perfect target for the insurgents' weapons!

SUNDANCE: DEATH IN THE LAVA
John Benteen

The Modoc's captured the wagon train and its cargo of gold. But now the halfbreed they called Sundance was going after it . . .

HARSH RECKONING
Phil Ketchum

Five years of keeping himself alive in a brutal prison had made Brand tough and careless about who he gunned down . . .

FARGO: PANAMA GOLD
John Benteen

With foreign money behind him, Buckner was going to destroy the Panama Canal before it could be completed. Fargo's job was to stop Buckner.

FARGO: THE SHARPSHOOTERS
John Benteen

The Canfield clan, thirty strong were raising hell in Texas. Fargo was tough enough to hold his own against the whole clan.

PISTOL LAW
Paul Evan Lehman

Lance Jones came back to Mustang for just one thing — revenge! Revenge on the people who had him thrown in jail.

HELL RIDERS
Steve Mensing

Wade Walker's kid brother, Duane, was locked up in the Silver City jail facing a rope at dawn. Wade was a ruthless outlaw, but he was smart, and he had vowed to have his brother out of jail before morning!

DESERT OF THE DAMNED
Nelson Nye

The law was after him for the murder of a marshal — a murder he didn't commit. Breen was after him for revenge — and Breen wouldn't stop at anything . . . blackmail, a frameup . . . or murder.

DAY OF THE COMANCHEROS
Steven C. Lawrence

Their very name struck terror into men's hearts — the Comancheros, a savage army of cutthroats who swept across Texas, leaving behind a bloodstained trail of robbery and murder.

SUNDANCE: SILENT ENEMY
John Benteen

A lone crazed Cheyenne was on a personal war path. They needed to pit one man against one crazed Indian. That man was Sundance.

LASSITER
Jack Slade

Lassiter wasn't the kind of man to listen to reason. Cross him once and he'll hold a grudge for years to come — if he let you live that long.

LAST STAGE TO GOMORRAH
Barry Cord

Jeff Carter, tough ex-riverboat gambler, now had himself a horse ranch that kept him free from gunfights and card games. Until Sturvesant of Wells Fargo showed up.

McALLISTER ON THE COMANCHE CROSSING
Matt Chisholm

The Comanche, McAllister owes them a life — and the trail is soaked with the blood of the men who had tried to outrun them before.

QUICK-TRIGGER COUNTRY
Clem Colt

Turkey Red hooked up with Curly Bill Graham's outlaw crew. But wholesale murder was out of Turk's line, so when range war flared he bucked the whole border gang alone . . .

CAMPAIGNING
Jim Miller

Ambushed on the Santa Fe trail, Sean Callahan is saved by two Indian strangers. But there'll be more lead and arrows flying before the band join Kit Carson against the Comanches.

GUNSLINGER'S RANGE
Jackson Cole

Three escaped convicts are out for revenge. They won't rest until they put a bullet through the head of the dirty snake who locked them behind bars.

RUSTLER'S TRAIL
Lee Floren

Jim Carlin knew he would have to stand up and fight because he had staked his claim right in the middle of Big Ike Outland's best grass.

THE TRUTH ABOUT SNAKE RIDGE
Marshall Grover

The troubleshooters came to San Cristobal to help the needy. For Larry and Stretch the turmoil began with a brawl and then an ambush.

WOLF DOG RANGE
Lee Floren

Will Ardery would stop at nothing, unless something stopped him first — like a bullet from Pete Manly's gun.

DEVIL'S DINERO
Marshall Grover

Plagued by remorse, a rich old reprobate hired the Texas Trouble-shooters to deliver a fortune in greenbacks to each of his victims.

GUNS OF FURY
Ernest Haycox

Dane Starr, alias Dan Smith, wanted to close the door on his past and hang up his guns, but people wouldn't let him.

DONOVAN
Elmer Kelton

Donovan was supposed to be dead. Uncle Joe Vickers had fired off both barrels of a shotgun into the vicious outlaw's face as he was escaping from jail. Now Uncle Joe had been shot — in just the same way.

CODE OF THE GUN
Gordon D. Shirreffs

MacLean came riding home, with saddle tramp written all over him, but sewn in his shirt-lining was an Arizona Ranger's star.

GAMBLER'S GUN LUCK
Brett Austen

Gamblers seldom live long. Parker was a hell of a gambler. It was his life — or his death . . .

ORPHAN'S PREFERRED
Jim Miller

Sean Callahan answers the call of the Pony Express and fights Indians and outlaws to get the mail through.

DAY OF THE BUZZARD
T. V. Olsen

All Val Penmark cared about was getting the men who killed his wife.

THE MANHUNTER
Gordon D. Shirreffs

Lee Kershaw knew that every Rurale in the territory was on the lookout for him. But the offer of $5,000 in gold to find five small pieces of leather was too good to turn down.